The Preludes

a novel by

John Caedan

West Winter Press

Large Format Paper Edition
Continuous Printing
First Published May 15, 2014

Library of Congress
Control Number: 2014936947

ISBN: 9780983857549

Published by West Winter Press

Twelve Days

Extras

Marked with a diamond: ♦

Extra scenes may be accessed at
appropriate moments in the story.
As they occur, they are marked with
a diamond and the page number on
which they may be found.

Occurrences of music are also marked
with a diamond as the story progresses.
To listen, visit the "music page" at
http://thepreludes.com

Prologue

Only at the zenith of the sun's transit north did it reach position, once a year for several days only, to throw long first rays against the north face of the building this way. It was dawn in midsummer. Already the façade glowed golden and now another tower's shadow slipped down to let the sun burst through the north-facing sheet of glass on the top floor.

This rare solstice fire set alight the south wall of a bright room. A canvas hung there. The painting seized its share of sunlight and devoured it. Into ferocious reds went the heat, into long crimson slashes went the scintillating brilliance, into the incessant layering of hue roiling through magenta and orange to the edge of yellow so pale it burned white hot went the power of the sun falling to earth.

A man slept beneath the painting sprawled on a jet-black sofa, head wedged between pillows, the straight brown hair-strands against vermillion covers the only shade of moderation in the room. In a streak, in one second, he rose upright on the floor, sheet streaming away from his naked body, his form still again, motion lost in the room.

One arm hung straight down. It was extraordinary. Beneath the skin the muscles stretched taut in defined ropes twining down the length, below the elbow forming a solid mass, tapering, the forearm nearly the thickness and heft of a baseball bat. At the wrist began the expanse of a remarkable hand, fully nine inches high, arched and shaped now in an expression of power.

Set in a defiant face, wide-open eyes burned with intent. There was not the slightest sign sleep had tamed him.

He raised his face to the painting. Its force washed over him. A flicker of recognition flashed in his eyes. Against this the lids narrowed, the skin over the forehead drew taut and he jerked around to find the object of fixation in this room, dominating it, an immense and imposing grand piano, ebony, gleaming inside with polished brass. In five swift strides he reached the keyboard.

At once music filled the room, a lonely repeated note poised on a knife edge, then a ragged figure with a melody slicing through as if renting the wild wind. Repeatedly he pulled from the deepest bass four octaves to the top, crashing back through the arpeggios of the half-saddened key, pierced by the melody, an utterance above the storm.

It was his Prelude No. 1, written in the night. It fell to the bottom of the keyboard, reaching the end on a low note, profound, dark, final.

♦ Prelude No. 1 ♦
to listen, go to the music page at thepreludes.com

Thursday

At the end of summer Georg Wojciechowski's purpose as a composer found him marching swiftly up the west side of Columbus Avenue in New York City in conversation with his friend Mark, an energetic black American opera singer, twenty-three years old, along for the mission so they could talk. They approached Lincoln Center with Mark effusive over his near-future plans.

"... and after Boston, the audition in L.A., then off to Santa Fe by car, maybe. Yieeee what a tromp. Damned expensive. I don't care. This is it, Georg, I am in play." He made a little skip step, hopping to his excitement. His trip would kick off in a week and a day with a Friday morning flight to Boston.

"You are going to be booked out two years by Christmas," Georg responded. "I predict it. Which part do you want most?"

"Marcello in *La Bohème* at City Opera of Los Angeles next April.

"COLA they call themselves, right?" said Georg.

"That's right. Or 'City Opera' for short. I found out it's not been cast yet, amazingly. There was a scheduling mix-up."

"Is that actually realistic in L.A.?"

"Well, COLA is a hot, ambitious opera company, they are friendly competitors with Los Angeles Opera, so there will be many guys trying for that role. It's unusual for such an important part not to be nailed down this late."

"So, is it realistic?"

"Okay okay I might need payola," Mark admitted, comically exasperated.

They turned left around the corner of the New York State Theater and entered Lincoln Center Plaza. The fountain's garrulous eruptions joined the wind blowing numerous banners, imparting to the scene a fresh, vigorous atmosphere.

"I will be in any city for your opening night. Anywhere," Georg promised.

"When I get in the company at City Opera I'm going to sublet a beach condo in Santa Monica and get a permanent tan."

Georg would only muster a grim smile and shake of the head at this typical Mark stab at preposterous irony. They continued their march diagonally across the main plaza in silence. Finally, right in front of the Metropolitan Opera House, Georg lost restraint. A blustering laugh escaped him.

"That's right," crowed Mark, "really tan and I don't burn." Mark's skin was the color of melted dark chocolate in a blackout.

Georg and Mark briskly turned the corner of the opera house into the north square of Lincoln Center. The Vivian Beaumont Theater stood to the left, Avery Fisher Hall to the right. Recessed between the Vivian and the Met sat their target, the Performing Arts Library, fronted by a black static steel sculpture by Alexander Calder.

Approaching the Calder Georg's attention fell on a man walking purposefully, perpendicular to his line of sight directly ahead, attempting to overtake someone near the sculpture, about twenty-five feet in front of Georg. The man reached this person, an Asian woman attired in a business suit, long black hair spilling down her back. Something in the woman's way of moving made Georg slow down. He put out his hand to signal Mark to slow also.

"Miss Lin, Miss Lin, I can't stand the way we left it, let

me try to convince you one more time," the man pleaded.

The woman stopped, turned to face him and provisionally offered her attention. Her petitioner thought they had semi-privacy but his voice echoed out from an overhang-created sound cave at the side of the theater building.

"You have to understand, it's the principle," he continued. "Your offer is below pay scale; it rubs the wrong way. Our people are so loyal to their union. They can't go against contract. What gets me is that you're from the People's Republic of China and you think the unions here have too much power? As your philosophical position? That's completely backwards," the man argued.

"Not everyone from China is a communist."

This comment brought Georg fully to a halt. Mark stopped beside him. The woman could not see them. The agent, too upset to care, resumed his case.

"Well, I just don't understand how you can expect us to bring Atlantic Dance Theater, yes we're small and new but we're making waves, I know you are attracted to that, how can you expect us to come to China without the official sponsorship of your government and leaving our union scale and stipulations behind?"

"Raw free trade," she immediately parried. "Value for value. I've got the clearances, the audience and the guaranteed funds. You have the popular young company. Let's trade."

"Look. I don't want to fight," the man countered. "This is Lincoln Center for goodness sake. And we really want this trip to China. Some of the dancers cried when they heard about the possibility. We can't seem to get a China trip through normal channels. Yet. But I have to say … you've got cowboy ideas, Miss Lin. The cowboys are dead; things are civilized now, we do things through government sponsorship, always, and every member of the company has a stake. I am in management and even I believe in the union with a passion," he finished.

"As an inducement I would pay you in gold, but you made that illegal when you killed all us cowboys."

Georg could not control a quick burst of laughter.

Lin spun around and noticed him for the first time. They locked eyes for a loaded, thrilling second. It was like looking into the face of Joan of Arc on a battlefield. The eyes were deep rich brown, nearly black. She swiveled back to face her adversary.

The man from the ballet took her by the arm in an effort to draw her away from Georg and Mark. "Let's go back to my office where we can speak in private. It's only two blocks."

"You have to say something brilliant and new for this conversation to continue."

The man could only sputter, "The dancers ... for them. For your country ..."

Silence. The woman's face remained stony. She waited politely, however. The agent tried a desperate final strategy.

"How are you going to explain to your people that you turned down the hottest new ballet company in the world? Over money?"

With great dignity Lin brought her hands together in front of her body, bowed slightly to him with mystery attitude, mock polite dismissal and veiled animosity. Slowly, with sing-song ceremony in highly-inflected Mandarin, she proclaimed loudly:

"*Lin Xin Qian.*"

The agent took a shocked step back. His eyes grew large. Finally he turned and awkwardly stomped away, disgusted and angry.

The woman turned her eyes on Georg.

"Maybe a tour around Greenland would make the dancers stop crying," he offered. "And cool them off."

Lin flashed a brilliant smile ... and then it was gone.

"Did you want to say that to his face?" she asked.

"Yes. It would seem to match your ironic cowboy speech."

"I am proud to be a cowboy."

"Apparently," Georg said with a laugh.

"I feel avenged for his insults. I fought him off with my ultimate argument."

"Was that a deadly Chinese swear word?"

"No, my name."

"Your name?"

"Yes."

"Fighting with only your name? Isn't that high danger?"

"With him, no ... with you, more so," she said, sounding matter of fact.

"Why?"

"You actually could be my enemy whereas he cannot affect me."

They seemed oblivious to Mark but he didn't care, watching with fascination.

Georg tested her once more.

"There is something at risk, here on the plaza of Lincoln Center?"

"Everywhere."

Georg lived with that for a moment, taking her in. She stood tranquil, comfortable in her body, sharply alert. They continued to hold each other's gaze.

Then, he attempted her name, "lin-shen-shan."

She corrected respectfully, "lin-shin-chien."

His second try was better, "Lin Xin Qian."

Then, adopting her power tone but perhaps not as grandiloquently, he issued his rejoinder: "Georg Maurycy Ignace Wojciechowski, Americanski."

"Yiiiiii. That would scare everyone in China. You could win fights with such a name. But you are American?"

"Yes. I am an American composer. This is my friend Mark, he is a tenor."

Nodding graciously, Mark announced himself with uninflected irony.

"Mark Warren Williamson."

Georg and Lin laughed over this incredibly American name and his flat delivery of it.

"Yes, I know," Mark offered, "I am not intimidating anyone with that. My weapon of choice is everything above G-sharp."

Lin nodded to Mark in acknowledgment of a good answer. Her black hair flowed and flitted in the breeze. Georg froze on purpose for a second, the better to feel pleasure flooding as when a new melody rose in him; the heart waiting for she whose aspect would thrill melted open for this exotic face. With the taste of daring in his mouth, he produced his business card, offering it to Lin.

"Would you come to Central Park South tomorrow at four o'clock to continue this conversation?"

Her face sobered, liquid eyes challenging his confidence. "What makes you think I would want to see you tomorrow?"

"For the surprise of discovering that I am more on your side than you are," Georg responded, imitating her matter-of-fact tone.

"That is doubtful. You have to say something brilliant and new for me to see you tomorrow."

A delicious knot of risk blossomed in his middle: to discover if the bloom of heat he sensed rising in her were real or existed only in his incited imagination.

"Something Wild West, something on a scale with your offer of gold to that gentleman?"

"At least," she said, taking the card provisionally, pinched between two fingers, staring him down with eyes wide.

"Compulsory taxation is slavery," Georg declared.

Lin shot a glance at Mark and back to Georg. A curtain descended in her eyes. With a slight bow, which they returned, she walked past them. They watched until she disappeared around the corner of the Metropolitan Opera House.

♦ Mark/Georg Discussion, page 133 ♦

Friday

The piano thundered out massively, the pianist immoderate. This was no song, no idyll, no turn of the heart. If a narrative obtained, it must be frightening. Yet at no point could the music be thought ugly, for the surety of justified anger never wavered. Accordingly, the ear bore the struggle, waiting to hear the bitter seed at the root of the tumult, begging the originator of such drama to reveal it.

Georg could not speak that seed. He was composing with full expectation the piece would expose it even as conflict accelerated, yet no breakthrough came. He made many forays, progressing, retreating, repeating, edging out, getting stuck.

At one point he took refuge from the piano at a window, breathing hard, interiorizing and then calming. He drank some water. His face reflected intensity but no fear.

With a jolt he returned to the keyboard. Several times he launched playback of his progress since his acoustic piano was also digitally-enabled and a laptop rested nearby. The music, though unresolved, was violent, dense, brilliant. And beautiful.

Then an interruption: his doorman buzzing on the intercom.

"What?"

"Sorry to disturb you, Mr. Wojciechowski, I've got a guest here who says she has an appointment with you."

"What? Who?"

"A Miss Zinchen, she's got your card."

Annoying the butchering of the name, *annoying* the early appearance – the clock spit 3:16 at him – *annoying* the need to not scream out loud.

"Okay Allen, let her come up."

Georg slanted across to the entryway leading to his elevator vestibule and cracked the door open, then turned his back on it all, taking the reverse angle back to the piano bench. The furious assault resumed. No fewer stops and starts than previously, no less jolting repetitions and detours filled the room as if the frustrations of Sisyphus.

The apartment door, through which the grumble of music must be flowing, opened quietly and Lin eased in. Apprising herself of circumstances she picked a spot on the farther of two sofas, about eighteen feet from the piano, out of all but the edge of peripheral vision of Georg. Off came her shoes, up into a curl went her form, legs under.

Lin witnessed twenty minutes of the struggle at the keyboard. She did not stir. Along the entire west side of the salon – to her left as she sat – fabric hung suspended, not opaque enough to block out all light, but enough that she could not see through. Behind her a pure white wall supplied the backdrop for the painting of the sun with its outpouring of outrageous color. A bar and utility area stood to her right. She only noticed this setting faintly; her focus lay inward, the bravura music calling upon her highest faculties.

Then, silence. Lin's focus sharpened. Georg sat perfectly still. His straight brown hair with tinges of amber lay across one side of a face drained of physical concentration yet still intensely serious, the slant of his high cheeks and mouth firm. It was a face inherited from ancestors in Eastern Europe. Often, as now, it wore the rough stubble of their beards. His nose was not to be ignored, handsomely dominant with a bump along its slope, not ignored unless one became wholly captivated by light-green eyes set under a strongly arched brow. Not to be ignored either, an erect carriage at the piano; this must be the result of endless hours in position, impossible to sustain without having developed a powerful core.

Georg stood and shot to a nearby table to retrieve a glass of water, returning to the keyboard, reaching for a phone sitting conveniently adjacent his workstation at the piano.

Perhaps, Lin believed, one might momentarily dis-remember the masterful seated posture when its owner moved: quick, purposeful, fluid. Arresting, like watching a dancer late to the barre.

The phone was on speaker and the sound of automatic dialing resounded into the room.

"Hello," came the greeting.

"This is Georg, professor."

"Ah Georg, you are well?"

"I'm calling not in a calm moment, but in the throes."

"I see."

"Do you have a moment?"

"Go ahead, Georg. What is the situation?"

"It's the new prelude. Far more intense than the last two."

"Major or minor?"

"It's in A minor, Professor Soebel, a war at the edge of melody. A melody can't come out, but keeps trying to. I don't want it to come out, I mean. But we hate empty noise."

"We hate empty noise, yes."

"I keep hearing that edict echoing in my head."

"My voice or yours?"

"You infected me forever and it is incurable," laughed Georg.

"So I am off the hook?"

"Yes."

The two men shared a fine chuckle. Then, a meaning-ful, thoughtful silence. Georg touched the keyboard affec-tionately without playing a note.

"Let me ask it this way," Soebel said. "Are you decon-structing A minor itself?"

"Close. Very chromatic. But hanging on to tonality."

"Perhaps it is an etude."

"Oh!"

"Let it be an etude. In other words, just a study, not a concert piece. Follow your instinct to keep melody locked up. Go all the way down that road. If it is indeed an etude and not a prelude, you will digest the insides of A minor. You won't let an etude onto the recital hall stage. But you don't know its actual fate, it might become something else. Let it be true to itself. You will find out."

"I can't believe how right you are. I'm speechless."

"How strong is the drive to compose this piece?"

"Immense."

"My work here is finished," Soebel said with irony.

"Beyond wisdom. Thank you," said Georg, hanging up on the call.

Georg sat down with a thump. He flipped settings on his controls to assure his workstation would continue to record everything to come. Then he attacked.

The *Etude in A Minor* slammed into place from beginning to end in one triumphant take. It was loud, aggressive, unapologetically tonal yet devoid of any central melody line. Always it threatened to spiral out of control. The composer, having risked the edge, proved it would not.

Finishing, Georg stood up at the keyboard, breathing hard. He clicked the mouse-control a few times. The system fed the recorded information back to the piano precisely, verbatim, and the etude erupted into the room, keys and pedal movements exactly as laid down. Georg walked behind the piano, his back to the room. Perfectly still, he listened all the way through while the giant piano played itself. At the end he remained intent and motionless in the enveloping silence for several long minutes.

Eventually he stirred and walked to the middle of the salon where Lin, now standing, offered her presence. They held each other's eyes.

"This was the moment of birth?" she asked.

"Yes."

"I came early on purpose, looking for you off-balance. I was willing to be told to come back later. I hope you will pardon. I did not expect to see this."

"It was a close call. If you'd made a sound or movement to disturb me, you'd have been shown the door."

"I know."

"How long were you sitting there?"

"Well, nearly forty minutes."

"I don't suppose you have any idea why I let you see this, do you?" asked Georg with a sweeping gesture toward the piano.

"Yes, I do. For the same reason I sensed it would be permitted to arrive early."

"Well?"

Lin paused. Her manner and expression turned mysterious.

"I want to remain unspoken on that," she said. "We should do everything off-balance."

In Georg's eyes the challenge was accepted.

"Tell me how your mother looked and felt when she explained your full name to you."

"I asked her many times."

"Yes?"

"There was one time, however, a special day. I was six. We were in the garden of our house. It was 1976, an enormous year of change in China, the death of Mao Zedong and Zhou Enlai, plus an earthquake that killed hundreds of thousands. Hundreds of thousands. But my mother was joyous that day, and I was not concerned with these happenings. She told me to put on a certain blue outfit I loved, one I was not allowed to show outside the house. She said 'Today we will walk in the city dressed in blue silk. Today Father will not go to the factory. Never again. He will return to his books, to the university, and we are Xin today.' She said that word like it was my name. I looked in her eyes and saw her crying and loving. She looked beautiful."

"I don't quite understand."

"In our language, with the correct tone, the name Xin means 'happy'."

"I see."

"You must say it: lin … shin … chien."

"Lin Xin Qian" said Georg carefully.

"Yes," she replied.

"What about 'Lin' and 'Qian', what do they mean?"

" 'Lin' is the name of my clan and comes from the idea of woods or forest. I will draw you the ideogram."

Georg led her to a side table, from the drawer of which he fished out a pad of watercolor paper and a felt marker. Lin swiftly and confidently drew the double-ideogram of the Lin clan.

"... like two trees," she whispered.

Georg's eyes were down, inspecting the florid drawing, but Lin's were on his face, studying him closely. When he raised his face to her, nodding in understanding, she looked in his eyes intently.

"I will tell you the meaning of 'Qian' if you ever say it to me in English."

Smiling at her way of play, he acquiesced. "Okay. But what shall I call you this evening?"

"Please, 'Lin.' It amuses me because some people think it is an American first name, short for Linda, that I have put on myself to 'belong' and I do not mind making it easy for everyone. But I hear it only as an echo of what it means in China. You can say it with that meaning also."

"Lin," he said.

"Yes. Just do not ever call me Linda Wong."

This caused them to break into laughter. Georg put his hand on her forearm. She did not shrink from his touch.

"How have you come to own this place?" she wanted to know.

"Wait ..." Georg responded, then walked to the west wall and activated a control. Smoothly, fabric slid away from the entirety of the west band of windows to reveal a terrace deck open to the sky with a fifty-foot lap pool oriented north-south along the very edge of the building. A hot water spa occupied the northwest corner. Beyond the edge of the terrace a spectacular view to the south, west and north of New York City exploded thrillingly.

Lin did not say a word. She shook her head and spread out her hands in an expression of shock. She looked over to him with inquiry.

"I have an aunt. Aunt Lydia, as a matter of fact. My grandmother's sister."

"Aunt Lydia is glorious."

"Lin, there's another whole floor below. This is a duplex. Thirty-seventh and thirty-eighth floors."

"Waaaaaah!" she wailed.

"That is Chinese swearing?"

"Cantonese astonishment. I speak Mandarin for business, but if you make me swear it will be in Cantonese."

Lin stared at the pool with desire. He was a little disappointed she did not jump in instantly, clothes and all. That would have been certainly off-balance. They walked out onto the terrace along the pool and stopped at the north edge of the building. All of Central Park lay at their feet. Georg waited until she looked in his eyes again.

"The Christians say it is harder for a rich man to enter the Kingdom of Heaven than for a camel to go through the eye of a needle. My benefactor Lydia makes it harder for me to earn this than either of those."

"I understand. The piano?"

"Aunt Lydia."

"The furniture and paintings? This enormous one with exciting colors?" she asked, indicating the canvas hanging on the white south-end wall of the salon area.

"Aunt Lydia. She is a music lover and art collector. Did you notice the gallery off to your left when you came in?"

"Yes."

"She's in Rome now for the shoulder season. Drives up to Florence all the time."

"Give me one or two sentences about her lineage."

"She is from the business and merchant world of Poland for many generations before her. When much of the family fled the old world, she didn't go to Ohio with the others. She and her husband made their fortune in New York real estate. She is bitter about things that happened in Poland, even before Hitler. But she, like me, embraces a certain romanticized version of Polish culture. We blame Chopin."

"I know him. Frédéric Chopin. Officially he is thought

too bourgeois in China, but privately his music is very much liked."

"Yes. Frédéric, the Pole of Paris."

Both smiling at that irony, they moved inside to the small bar area at the eastern wall of the salon.

"One more fact. Lydia owns this entire building itself, less ownership of many floors sold as condominiums."

"Astonishing," Lin said.

"The rest of my situation can be told easily. My father died while stationed in Saigon, when I was an infant. I was brought up in Ohio by my mother and extended family, but they sent me to study and live here in 1982 when I was twelve, watched over by Lydia and her husband Piotr."

Lin's gaze drifted to the side, picturing it.

"What happened with that person from Atlantic Dance Theater?" Georg asked. "Do you want some wine?"

Nodding to the offer, Lin responded.

"I must tell you why I am here, in the United States."

"Are you sure you don't want to talk about the mistakes of farmers in Patagonia? Or go ice skating on roller skates?"

"I am an ambassador," she said, deflecting his cleverness.

"Oh."

"Georg, before I tell you more, say what you said, again."

He knew full well to what she was referring; it had been hanging in the air between them the entire time.

"Compulsory taxation is slavery."

"You said that with Mark standing right there? Slavery?"

"He agrees with me. But only after a lot of really intense conversations over the last three years. I am thirty, he is twenty-three, but he's my best friend."

"I am thirty-one. So you both believe compulsory taxation is slavery. I will put to you the outrages."

"Fire away."

"You want freedom to make money and keep it all, but reject your responsibilities to the country that gives it to you."

"No one gives a human being freedom; it's part of being alive. That includes freedom to make wealth and keep it."

"What about your responsibilities?"

"I'm responsible for providing for my needs, paying my way, not inflicting burden on anyone else."

"What about people who can not pay their way?"

"Do not force me to help them. Persuade me. I am generous."

"What about being a citizen, about running the country, though?"

"I'd pay voluntarily, a share."

"Voluntary taxes?"

"Cut the current mess by about seventy percent. Here's how: get rid of all corporate welfare, but also corporate interference. That means, get rid of the fiat monetary system by privatizing money and backing it with gold, not government chits backed by the promise to tax my grandchildren. Don't subsidize business, but remove the shackles, bridles and hobbles from enterprise, large and small. Get out of the fucking way. The result will be an abundance and prosperity unimaginable now. Then, gradually get government out of the social programs completely. People will be able to pay their own way, or if truly unable will receive generous help voluntarily, which is the way it used to be. Then, take the remaining budget and call it the commons. Divide it by the number of adult citizens. Every person pays their commons voluntarily and they all pay the same amount. Unfortunate people will find family or benefactors to pay their commons for them, partially or fully, one year or many. No compulsory taxation."

"You are the right of me," Lin stated. She looked stunned.

"Not every artist is a communist," he said.

"Almost all artists would denounce the position you just described. Almost every person on earth would denounce it, I would say. What happened to you?"

"Lydia and my family infected me. I think better of

people than that everyone needs to be told what to do and that they can't make their own way."

"Are you optimistic?"

Georg shook his head.

"Many people want to hedge, to deflect absolute personal responsibility and strike a bargain to be taken care of by law, to some extent, in exchange for them owing legal obligation to others, and the entrenched power structure is more than happy to oblige, by law, and bind citizens to each other as duty. I am not optimistic that can or will change."

"But comparing taxes to slavery. With a great beautiful African-American standing right there? He is beautiful."

"Yes he is. People think their rage at actual human involuntary servitude is enough. There's a glow of goodness, they are in no mood to think anything else is needed to assure freedom. They give a free pass to the notion of involuntary servitude of money. Mark knows why I condemn both. He does too. In some ways, Mark is to the right of me!"

"Really?"

"Gets him in trouble all the time."

A pause. Georg poured more wine. They walked back out onto the terrace to stand against a railing with the view looking north through Central Park. Although the last day in August, breezes stirred occasionally that belonged to mid-summer. The pause grew longer. As opposed to becoming strained, they softened, fitting into each other's ways. Glances did not dart away.

"I am not a state ambassador," Lin said at just the right moment.

"No?"

"There is an ironic saying in my country. 'Communism with Chinese characteristics.'"

"Yes, very ironic."

"I am an ambassador from the characteristic of free enterprise."

"Are you rich and glorious?"

"My family is. I will give you the short version, for now. I am traveling for my uncle. He is a banker. We own a lot of land, developing it into communities. It is completely off the official table. We do not pay taxes on the profit."

"What?"

"I knew that would shock you."

"What?"

"But no help from the government either. No state bonds or cash infusions. They send officials everywhere into all our projects to be sure we are not raising up counter-revolutionaries or charging people forty percent. But as long as we put the profits back to development, they leave us alone, the apparent Chinese characteristic of looking past ideology to do what works."

"Outrageous. You are operating all this outside of control of the Communist apparatus?"

"Yes."

"Why? How can it happen?"

"Well, it is not really outside their control, since they observe and regulate everything, but it is on the outside of their money control, as I explained."

"But why the hell would they allow that?"

"We are building a part of the New China for them; they do not have to do a thing except stay out of the way and be sure we never challenge their authority. We get people off the 'net receiver' end of communism so officials do not have to take care of them, with only the cost that my family is less of a 'net provider' to the actual government treasury."

"I find this fascinating. Do you have pull or something?"

"The world does not know … there are whole networks of hundreds of entrepreneurs in our situation, mostly away from Beijing. It is not just houses, we are building infrastructure, shops, manufacturing facilities, all on handshakes, all with the communists pretending we do not exist. Not to mention direct banking. It is billions and vast."

Georg took a sip of wine, contemplating this startling information, looking out over the park for long moments.

"Do you still have the blue silk dress?"

"Yes. It is in a wooden chest with other things from my

childhood. My daughter will have them some day."

"Daughter?"

"Future daughter."

"Do you have a lover, Lin Xin Qian?"

"No." Then after a meaningful pause she added, "I detect no scent of perfume here."

"No."

They lingered over that for a minute, each looking often into the face of the other.

"You'll give me the longer version soon? Off the grid, tax-free?"

"Yes."

"I have to say something, actually to warn you."

"Yes?"

"I am bringing a project to the boil, preludes, *Ten Preludes for Piano*. Do you know what those are?"

"Yes, although I am not a musician, I have education in Western classical music. I like it tremendously."

"Earlier today," Georg continued, "I made a decision about them, to go for a public performance much sooner than I thought. Mark pushed me on my opera, but this premiere of *The Preludes* is more important. I made some phone calls. I have a date, a venue at the Chrystie Street Repertory Theater and the beginnings of a publicity plan to make a performance of them."

"Should I leave?"

"I would like you not to leave. But my drive at the piano can take over at any time. Also, there is some stress."

"It cannot be that you do not think your music is good enough."

"No, it's … something else. I'm working it out, but meanwhile, I can be pretty obsessed. I can part the curtains for a play or dinner with friends, but otherwise it is full-forward, at any moment day or night. I am gladly on pause now, though."

"To talk to me?"

"Yes."

"But you are feeling it call you now."

"Yes."

"So, normally, I would leave at some point so you can go monomaniac at the keyboard?"

"Yes, normally. I swear your English is really amazing, idiomatically, although sometimes it's just slightly off. Very endearing."

"I request correction when it is a little off. That will not spoil the charm for you, will it?"

"Not at all."

"Someone called me a monomaniac once and I looked it up. I liked it. Well, if your curtains are parted and you asked me to come here, why are you warning me about your obsessed behavior?"

"Even if I am on an official break from composing, if I can put the break itself on pause to run to the keyboard here and there, this can last a lot longer."

"What this?"

"This great zigzaggy conversation. I am suggesting a flow. A running conversation. Off-balance."

"This is something I like."

"Would you like to stay here around the clock?" he asked, only realizing how daring it sounded after saying it. "I have plenty of room for you."

"I had not planned on marriage today," she responded, deadpan.

"We can call it the strivers' co-op of the thirty-eighth floor."

"If I tell you this feeds into my own plans …?"

"It does?"

"I have a major presentation to prepare, which I must deliver a week from Monday. Very major. No one to be at the meeting makes less than four hundred thousand dollars. I need the best possible accommodations to stay in while I work it up. Would you like to encounter someone with a focus as strong as yours?"

"You'll never match me."

"I am working right now, engine running at about fifteen percent."

"I'm playing that etude I just composed, inside right now. It's in my belly. To continue my warning … I've had trouble with this before. You can't take it as rude if a moment arrives and I go off to the keyboard oblivious of everything. I mean, it can happen at any random instant. One second I am talking with you, the next split second I am unreachable. By agreement, we are saying you will understand, not take it personally?"

"You should not even say 'excuse me for a minute.' "

"There is an idiom 'strike while the iron is hot.' That's what I have to do."

Lin nodded, then made an expressive circular motion with a hand.

"... and reverse?" she asked.

"I agree."

"So we can be zigzaggy. I have to look that up."

"How could such conditions be good for your plans?"

"I can work here. It is for my own reasons, I want to. A bold request, of course. Among other things, I want to swim in your pool ... at odd hours."

"I see," he said, not knowing the implication to be intentional by her or wishfulness by him. He didn't care, it was delicious.

"I just need a table."

"That's easy, take the big dining room table on the other side of the gallery."

Lin held out her hand toward him, palm up.

"If you would accept such a deferral, I will withhold the full explanation of why this would be better than my cave at the Sherry-Netherland Hotel. My reason is resting in the palm of my hand. You won't guess it; it is way off-balance."

"Okay."

"My engines just went up to twenty percent," she stated.

"What do you need to get set up?"

In a graceful gesture Lin slowly folded her arm back to her torso, closing her fingers. Looking into his eyes with a spark in hers she said just one word.

"Pajamas."

Georg's pool now had swimmers.

Lin's roller suitcase rested against an inside wall but she sat along the pool's north edge dangling feet in the water. It remained warm enough in the late afternoon for such swishing while wet and for swimming. Her suit was a sleek one-piece, black. Black as her hair. Both suit and hair shone brightly in the low-angle sunlight; she had just finished several laps. Georg stood at the far south end with New York arrayed around. He held a strategic pose momentarily but then entered the water in a shallow dive. His strokes up the lap pool stayed steady and purposeful. He did not make a turn at the end, instead halting to look up at Lin.

"Tomorrow."

"Yes?"

"It's Saturday, something I do a few times every month on Saturday, my piano project."

"What is it?"

"Up in the Bronx, place called Mozart Pianos, they are the best you'll find anywhere, restoration, rebuilding, refurbish."

"Mozart Pianos?"

"I know, their name is ridiculously on the nose, isn't it. Do you know that idiom?"

"Yes."

" 'Mozart Pianos' sends a blunt message, doesn't it, about being serious?"

"No Lewis Jerry Li whacking away!"

"How can you know that guy?" Georg asked, laughing.

"There was a movie about him, we saw it in China. He rattles the bones."

"Very amusing, the way you said his name."

"Chinese to American name wit."

"They have too many pianos, upright pianos."

"Really?"

"It's a sad reality, the pool of uprights is bigger than the demand. Once most houses in America had a piano and everyone played, but now few do. They might have an electronic piano, or the teens might have a synth with piano sample. No real flesh and blood wood and steel piano, though. Mozart Pianos actually has to dismantle uprights.

They stockpile the wood of the cabinets for use in their rebuilds."

"That *is* sad."

"I'm part of a project that tries to put the uprights into homes where there is a young musician. I think of it as avoiding piano dismemberment and looking for an unknown Artur Rubinstein. You can go with me if you want."

Georg made a strong push off the end of the pool and launched a racing lap. Remarkable, within two seconds his interior impressions while he swam were those driven by the music he was composing, not she who sat at pool's edge. He realized his swimming strokes coincided with the rhythm of his latest prelude; it accompanied him all the way down and back.

He stopped at the north end again and looked up at Lin. She continued to dangle her feet in the wonderful water.

"Perhaps and depends."

Georg nodded.

"What is a synth?" Lin asked.

Georg climbed out of the pool, put a hand down and pulled her upright. "I'll show you," he said.

They wrapped robes around themselves and he took her by the arm inside. He led her to the piano.

"This is a Bösendorfer."

"Yes?"

"It is the best piano in the world. It's like playing an orchestra."

"You certainly produce a prodigious noise with it."

"A prodigious meaningful noise."

They laughed over that. Lin took a towel from around her neck and used it to dry her long hair. Georg appreciated this activity in silence while drying himself off. He gradually became aware she knew he knew she knew he was reading everything into it. The flirting was subtle and loaded.

Georg picked up a pair of headphones. "But … it's wired. Watch."

He flipped open the laptop which rested on a desk next to the piano, then clicked and scrolled to activate the digital file that held his Prelude No. 7. The system drove the piano to play it, not only activating the keys but the pedals as well. Music filled the salon.

"Yes, like I saw earlier."

"I play it into the system, I save the performance in the computer, I run it back like this anytime so I can listen to the piano play itself."

"It is fantastic."

"Watch this," he said.

He flipped a switch. The keys continued to depress, but the sound ceased. Lin gave him a glance. Georg handed her the headphones, which she put on. Her eyes got big.

"Wowie!"

Georg laughed and stood back to let her listen. After a moment he clicked back on the computer and the playback ended.

"I want to hear the rest. What is that?"

"My newest prelude. I'm writing a sheaf of preludes. This is number seven. I worked on it all the time you were gone to get your things. What you heard earlier, the etude, I've put that away for now."

Her eyes heated up. "Can I hear the rest of this Prelude Number 7? It makes me catch my breath it is so tender."

"If you indeed stay here this weekend, you'll hear it many times. I am finishing it now. I'd say we have about ten minutes before it pulls me in like an undertow. There's food in the kitchen, have anything. I showed you where you can sleep downstairs. What are you going to do about the endless music? Are you sure this is a good idea?"

"You will not play by headphones if normally you would not." Lin stepped closer, inside his private space. "Do nothing unusual on my account."

Georg nodded with a look of finality.

"The sound in the headphones is good, but not the same as purely this beautiful instrument. What comes out of the headphones is a synthesized sound, made by a synth, which is hardware in the action of the keyboard and software in the computer. It does not affect the actual playing, but records and plays back exactly every move I make, as you have seen. When I flip this switch, the hammers are prevented from striking the strings, and the real sound is replaced by the synthesized sound played back through the headphones."

"I see. So someone can play on headphones at three-thirty in the morning as loud as desired."

"Yes. But I much prefer the actual acoustic sound of the actual piano. Up here, with windows closed, buffered by my floor below … I can play as loud as desired. At three-thirty in the morning."

Lin nodded understanding.

"Last warning," he said, simply.

"Do not hold back your intensity. That is one reason I came here, to be near it. To match it."

Georg made a nod of comradeship. Lin returned it.

As the sun went down Georg returned to work on the prelude. At times he could be seen eating a plum, getting a drink of water, flipping pages of printed-out music or slumping exasperated at the keyboard. At other times: joyously succeeding. There was no sign of him looking for Lin.

All during, she established her beachfront on the huge dining table two rooms away from the busy piano. She moved chairs out of the way and cleared the table of everything except charts and organizational notes arrayed around her laptop and a small travel printer. She made a phone call once.

She took another swim, also, at one point interrupting it at the north end of the lap pool where it met the roof line, affording a spectacular view out over Central Park. Back at the table, she paced and spoke into a hand-held voice recorder and also at times typed furiously into her computer.

Lin waited until it seemed Georg was on a break, based on him enjoying bread and cheese at the small bar area near the piano.

"May I speak?" she asked.

"Yes."

"I need a fairly large whiteboard. I was going to have one delivered to the Sherry for the weekend. Can I have it brought here?"

"That is not a problem. Tomorrow?"

"Yes."

"I'll tell the doorman in the morning to expect the delivery."

Lin thanked him and spun away. Later she could be seen enjoying a bowl of soup in the kitchen on the floor below, near her bedroom. Georg returned to his taste of baguette with Manchego. Later he lay prone under the piano with the prelude floating along, listening, feeling it.

One other thing could be seen just as the sun set: Lin's bed. A garment landed on it, still folded. Her arm and a sliver of her naked hip from the side were visible as she gracefully reached for the clothing, namely her pajamas.

Eventually Georg came to a break point. He sat at the piano for a long moment, digesting and settling. He stood and crossed the room to the farther of the two sofas. Lin sat curled up there.

"It is wonderful," she said.

♦ Prelude No. 7 ♦

"I'm done with it for the moment. It has to age a little now."

"You can just move emotion, directly."

Georg nodded. Lin seemed effected by the idea. "You choose where to move it and how."

"Yes. Emotion and the truth underneath the emotions. The realities."

"I have never been this close to the sourcing of such power in music."

Georg sat down next to her. She finished her compliment:

"It opens the heart."

"Thank you."

Lin gave a small bow of the head. They shared a verbal silence inhabited by the echoes of the final resolution of the music, which seemed to linger in the room with a life of its own.

"In order to control emotion and reality in your music like that, to open the heart, you must find it familiar. I mean, high emotion is not unusual to you."

"I have it in my hands, like a sculptor. There is a certain amount of the mundane, technique, practice, control—"

"—but then—"

"—but then there is the instant all mundane drops away and you have the living thing in your hands. With Romantic music, this sculpting of emotion carries a serious responsibility."

"Are you to be trusted with it?"

Georg leaned forward on this challenge. "When I play Chopin or Rachmaninov, they have been the source. It would not occur to me to betray them. Lin, they are playing, really. It is my duty to not hold back, nor to exploit. I have to honor their intent."

He paused to gather himself.

"When I play my music … each time … there is an additional kind of loyalty … that's as much as I can say. Wait, I'll say one more thing. For this music, Romantic music, I have to live up to the emotion."

"This is difficult."

"Yes. I have to live what I am saying. What I am evoking."

Lin nodded and they sat with this. The silence again was not strained but as well not trivial. Then she resumed.

"I have three tasks as ambassador. They involve moving people. May I tell you about them?"

"I've been waiting! You have my full attention. Let me hear the first part and then I'm going to get wine."

"I am here leading a team to strike a deal downtown. Our bank is ready to make bigger investments in China; we need capital. All next week the fund we are wooing has us on the carpet to provide our bona fides and run down every line of the business plan for the venture. I am armed with spreadsheets and allocation budgets, repayment history databases and lender profiles until I am up to the eyeballs."

They smiled together over her idiomatic deployment.

"We are very prepared. This deal is moving through. The hardest part is matching our unofficial cash flow with their fully transparent establishment corporate funding and profit taking."

"Oh."

"We had to test if it would throw up red flags and we had to engage certain American central bankers and securities watchdogs in passing on the transaction. We seem to have clear water ahead."

"This sounds big."

"First round, one point three billion U.S."

"Whoa."

"Yes. I am in awe of being at the center of such a transaction. When I concentrate on it I feel a humming in my head. My uncle has spoken of it as well, the potency of a billion dollars."

She paused. Georg believed she was feeling the potency. It made her keen.

"I will see to it that every cent gets put to work," she concluded resolutely.

"So at this moment I am speaking to the person directing one of the most important high-level capital transfers taking place in New York City?"

"Yes." Lin smiled and made a little dance motion, sitting there, as if to leave a splash of victory celebration hanging about her person.

"My second mission is cultural. For instance, as you saw yesterday, I am to open talks with the Atlantic Dance Theater for a tour to the interior, under the sponsorship of our own impresarios."

"A privately funded and produced tour not hosted by the Communist Government of the People's Republic of China?"

"Exactly." She paused dramatically. "This mission is in trouble."

Georg laughed heartily, having seen the debacle first hand. "Did the Atlantic guy demand to see your Communist Party membership card?"

Lin responded dryly. "Would it be your estimate that

I have marshalled my demonstrations of safety, approval, planning and finance, that I have cleared the way ahead of time?"

"I would bet my Bösendorfer that you are massively armed and ready."

"Apparently, my assurances are inadequate."

"No!"

"They are nervous operating outside the umbrella of government sanction."

"A ballerina might get caught in an unauthorized *pas de deux* with a Chinese Don Juan?"

"You should have heard the objections when I tried to make it a true cultural exchange, privately, to offer a reciprocal visit from a marvelous ballet company, a Western-style ballet company, from my own city of Wuhan. They don't like my financial offer either, even though it is guaranteed cash at about eighty-five percent of their normal compensation."

"You have other stories like this?"

Lin nodded with a wan smile of fake self-disappointment. "I am a failure as cultural attaché."

After a moment of mutual delight in this declaration, Lin moved on.

"It is the third mission …"

She stood up as if to face her troubles head-on, ready for battle. Georg got up to fetch a bottle of red wine and glasses and poured for them. He waited for her to begin.

"Georg, compulsory taxation *is* slavery at the deepest level. You and I are standing here, two crackpots, probably the only two people north of Wall Street who understand this and believe it. Who see the danger of money that is not free. How did we meet again?"

"I attended one of your fights."

"Money itself is enslaved. I have a front row seat in this. I am a citizen of Communist China, yet I am wheeling and dealing billions like a cowboy rounding up wild horses in Wyoming. But in New York, the world headquarters of capitalism, you can barely saddle up. Your money is controlled. There are so many regulations, tax implications, fairness requirements, shareholder advocacy lawyers, environmental strictures, class action lawsuit threats and most of all Federal Reserve controls on the money, it feels like you cannot spin around even to look at your transaction because you will break something with your elbow. The result is not free market enterprise, but a fixed game where the government operatives and corporate CFOs make a Frankenstein. That is a correct use of Frankenstein?"

"Yes," he laughed.

"The corporation magically receives relief from all these barriers, like the sea parting. It gets protection from competition, a certain level of pass-through on regulation and a green light by the authorities, while the government gets assurance of tax revenue, support for individual politicians and bureaucracies and the stamp of benevolence. It is not a business deal, really. One person on my team calls it 'a gigantic tarball birthed by the orthodoxy.' I had to look up 'tarball.' "

Georg chortled at this colorful description.

"Because it is a fixed game played with damaged money, it is bloated with unrealities and waste. Very often the result is something that should never have been born."

"There must be some honesty and actual fair exchange and mutual value for the players," Georg offered.

"Yes that is true, but still so much of American business is unnatural … there is something wrong in China too."

"Yes?"

"In my province in China we have the age-old problem of peasants and workers filled with resentment and often hate for businessmen, landowners and bankers. This attitude was made worse by the Communists who taught them to elevate their prejudices to the highest level of morality, to become proud warriors against the Bourgeoisie. They inflamed class hatred the same way Hitler inflamed race hatred. Mao Zedong used this to make a revolution.

"But now, in my lifetime, China is told to spin around completely, to be joyous when you get rich and to not hate others who already are rich, because this is how to make China a great nation in the world."

"Not because you have the absolute right to own your property—"

"—only because it serves the nation. It is your duty to get rich."

Lin was struck silent. Georg waited. They returned to sit on the sofa. It surprised him to see her near tears, rocking back and forth with her arms clasped around her knees. In her sorrow she was also shaking with rage. Lin let him see the pain in her eyes. When she spoke it was with force of courage and without suppressing grief.

"I do not believe in this government's version of 'democratic enterprise.' I do not trust the communists. And I am fucking furious."

There was no sign in Georg he was put off. He bent forward toward Lin and nodded quietly but did not touch her. He signaled availability with words.

"Why are you furious?"

Lin gathered her composure and retrenched.

"My presentation."

"Yes?"

"Monday I was at lunch with Henry Lane, the CEO of this corporation with which I am negotiating the capital funds. I said something off-balance."

Georg smiled at this allusion. Smiling was not in Lin, however.

"He latched onto it. The next time I looked up we had missed the *next* meal. Lane has a way of seizing upon important conceptions and running them down. Far down. His persistence and forceful ways were very impressive. It was thrilling, actually, to be put to such a test."

"You found out why he is CEO of an important corporation."

"Yes. In those five hours his roots got a direct injection of growth hormone. At least that is what he said at the end, something like that."

"Wow."

"He challenged me to present my thinking to his key executives. I immediately said yes; this is my third mission, after all, to look for ways to free up capitalism in the world.

We picked a date, which is the tenth of September, a week from Monday. He is flying in all his top people from around the country. Meanwhile, this coming week on Wednesday I will be meeting with him downtown to run through a progress draft of my intended presentation. Lane said he would tear it apart with me but also 'praise it and raise it' at the same time, make me go beyond even his sea change, until it is 'nothing short of nitroglycerine.' That was his word for it."

"Is this paid?" interjected Georg.

"Interesting that you ask. We had that discussion. Lane actually said 'I should pay you a million, or charge you a million for the opportunity.' I said 'a bargain in either case,' and I was quite serious. He is a cowboy too."

Georg smiled widely at this reference.

"We settled on us splitting the tab for dinner at the Four Seasons Wednesday night. I shall order a steak."

"That's excellent. It's still a fine restaurant, you go there to celebrate a big artistic or business deal, that's a tradition."

Lin kept her eyes on his steadily.

"You wanted to ask me, just now, if I went to bed with him."

"Yes."

"He signaled that he was married and that it was serious. And we are involved in a professional business transaction."

Georg looked directly at her, without reaction. Lin let a significant beat pass, then continued.

"Georg, I know everything I want to say to Lane's people. I have made this presentation several times before. This time, though, it is at a higher level. I am having a struggle letting it loose, letting it fly. My rage is in the way."

She looked at him with intention and inquiry. Georg understood at once.

"If you are concerned that this is too intense considering we just met each other, please let that pass. Let it out."

Lin looked long and hard into his eyes. She evidenced both risking and trust of him. What was even more certain: she could hold it in no longer.

"After the Japanese were driven away in 1945, my grandfather and his father retrieved their gold from hiding. They waited for stability, then put to work with others rebuilding Hubei Province. This was successful. And why not, my family and those like us had rebuilt central China many times in the same way for thousands of years.

"The next twenty years were ugly. First, there was Civil War. Then Mao Zedong drove the Nationalists off the mainland in '49 and began collectivizing farms during the early fifties. In '57 Mao broke off with the Soviet Union and ..." Lin could not continue immediately. Georg waited a moment, then helped.

"The Great Leap Forward. I have read about that."

"Yes. Georg, it was terrible. My family will not forget. We do not talk of it often, but no Lin grows to adulthood without the stories that the world has forgotten. Mao was a vicious brute. He enslaved the lives of a nation. Vast populations were taken off the farms and made to work in factories. Peasants no longer owned or rented their land; they worked under total coercion on land as slave laborers. Everything failed. Industries Mao attempted to force into production made nothing, or worse, made dangerous and useless things. The collective farms he tried to force to produce three times what they could, instead produced one-tenth what they should. My great-grandmother knew what it is to starve."

Lin's bitterness surfaced.

"Her child died in her arms. Millions of children died in their mothers' arms. And then the women themselves died. The displacements, the famine, the destruction of farm lands, the waste of savings and the despair nearly destroyed China. But the monster was not done."

She lashed out with fury at the memory. "Mao would have his purity, his Marxism-Leninism with Chinese characteristics."

Lin stood up, shuddering with agitation. Georg stood as well.

"In 1956 Mao allowed and encouraged Zhou Enlai to elicit intellectuals to give criticism of the government.

This was not met with enthusiasm. Mao then took over the campaign, attaching a poem with the phrase 'Let a hundred flowers bloom; let a hundred schools of thought contend' and ordered – ordered – intellectuals to voice their opinions, ostensibly to 'push the government toward the better' and 'encourage the growth of socialism.'

"Mao got his flood of criticism. Millions of letters, almost all derogatory and denouncing the government."

Lin paused to gather courage.

"My grandfather and his father wrote letters. They were landowners and bankers, yes, but they were community leaders and also wrote books and poetry and encouraged learning. They were forced to write the letters by local party cadres on threat of exile and transport to slave labor camps. In the spring of 1959 Mao sent special army regiments into our province. They were to enforce the will of his agents of purity, who soon followed. It was a purge."

"Oh no."

"As part of the Great Leap Forward, the entire structure of our district was dismantled and collectivized, including massive work reassignment and the confiscation of all of the remaining property of my family. Naturally all promises to repay loans to us were voided. The very idea of ownership of property was voided. My grandfather, my great-grandfather and his wife, a vocal poet, were harshly criticized and then formally charged with the crime of 'opposing Chairman Mao' because of their letters and with 'bourgeois exploitation' because of being landholders."

Georg stood face to face with Lin. Her visage was resolute, like a solder. He was not so controlled.

"On March 14th, 1959, along with seventy other 'criminals' who had been identified by the Hundred Flowers letters, my ancestors were herded into the public square. The entire town was assembled at gunpoint to witness. My great-grandmother would not go voluntarily. She was beaten, stripped naked and dragged by her hair. She was the first one shot, shot many times in limbs and left in agony before dying. The women were shot first and their bodies dragged into mud and mutilated. Their husbands were not shot immediately, the more to suffer as their loved ones were killed and humiliated in front of their eyes. Then they were tortured by forcing each to break the bones of others with metal rods, before each injury ordered to denounce themselves and apologize to the proletariat. However, no recant would be enough. Before dark there were seventy-three bodies in the square, shot through the head one by one over several hours, with the joyous communist cadres ordering the people to sing and celebrate the cleansing of their town."

She stopped, wide-eyed and heaving. Georg did not turn from the sight, but did not attempt any gesture of sympathy.

Lin cried out in indignation and rage.

"I protest the torture and execution of my ancestor Lin Zheng Li and his father Lin Bao and the poetess Lin Hua Wen."

She bent over, frozen by the force of it. She had held back not at all. The room crackled with electricity. Then Lin came erect and turned steely cold again.

"My father stood in the square that day, ten years old, weeping and terrified. He witnessed the humiliating suffering and slaughter of his father. He told me once, when I asked, that he could not look away at the moment his father's brains were blown out. My grandmother lay moaning in the mud next to him, traumatized and damaged forever. She had not been executed because she was pregnant.

"Naturally, my remaining family was under suspicion forever. My father was not allowed to attend secondary school, but rather forced into a collectivized rice farm at the age of thirteen. He was nearly murdered in 1966 when the Red Guard swept through Hubei Province. He was only saved because he had memorized the Little Red Book as a safety measure and denounced his father and all bourgeois ancestors in the most vociferous manner."

Georg asked, "Your father became a scholar …?"

Lin continued as if from a distance. "Mao's insanity fell out of favor. He was not deposed, but everything eased. The Cultural Revolution fizzled. My father was allowed to return home at age twenty-three in 1971. He brought with him his wife and two-year-old girl child."

"You."

Lin nodded grimly. Her pain was coming.

"He was made to work in a factory. As the fanaticism for purity waned, he quietly increased his reading of literature, old literature. He was permitted to go to university only in 1976, the day I wore my blue silk dress in the town."

Lin sank down to the carpet, kneeling, Georg likewise, half facing her and always unwaveringly holding her eyes when offered to him. Gradually, quietly, and then with increasing pathos, she began to weep.

"Georg, this man and this socialist philosophy killed ... millions of people in a few decades. People slaughtered ... starved, tortured. All lives ... ripped away from their happiness. Millions ... made into slaves."

Lin spoke no more. Sobbing possessed her, exhausted her and began to cleanse. Georg brought her water. He remained kneeling next to her until the pain subsided. Full release required the better part of an hour. Night descended, quelling all emanation from the painting of the falling sun that looked over the salon.

Finally, Lin's convulsions came to an end. She looked up at Georg. Her face was much changed.

"I must dare to ask you for something. I risk it."

"Ask me, Lin."

She stood, wobbly, and offered her hand. He grasped it. She walked them to the Bösendorfer.

"I need to sleep now, but if it is in your heart, play one thing. But not sad. Please show me something lovely and sweet."

Georg looked into her eyes ... then let go of her and moved to the piano bench. Lin's hand, with its pajama cuff, slowly lifted to grasp the wood of the cabinet. She held it there, to feel, during the next moments.

From the great piano came the sound of a new prelude, born that instant, simple, clean and full of hope.

Saturday

Georg and Lin came sailing out of their lobby into a spectacular September 1st day dressed in jeans, cotton tops, sweaters and athletic shoes, jumbling around, deciding which way to walk, in a happy mood.

"The Park!" Lin insisted.

"Well I have to get up to the Bronx."

"The Park!"

"Ay-yi-yi-yi-yi well here, let's take the path diagonally across, we can get a cab on Fifth Avenue."

They jaywalked across Central Park South and entered Central Park, taking the path east and north, passing both the amusement park and small zoo, in conversation all the while, soaking up air and sunshine. The leaves had not yet turned color but that transformation was certainly imminent.

"What was that you were playing this morning?"

"Carl Czerny."

"Is that somebody Polish?"

"He was Czech but born and lived in Vienna. All over the world pianists know the name of Carl Czerny but not one normal music lover does. He is only famous for fiendishly difficult but tremendously helpful exercises. I was playing from his *School of Velocity*."

"A most appropriate title!" laughed Lin. "I was brushing my teeth at a furious pace."

"I play him every day. Truth be told, I am not a genius pianist and performer but rather a composer. Sometimes I can't even play the pieces I compose."

Lin whispered to him: "Did you capture that piece you played for me last night?"

"Yes."

"Georg," she said, back in normal voice, "these pieces I am hearing, where are you going with them?"

"Well I've put together the elements of an event, namely the world premiere of these preludes. No one has heard any of them except my inner circle. To present a sheaf of preludes to the world is bold."

"How so?"

"The great Romantic composers did it, especially Chopin and Rachmaninov. Later, Claude Debussy. They make a statement, taken as a whole, about the foundation of the composer's commitment to … I want to say to an aesthetic … but it is more emotional than that, to a style and tone and meaning. To what makes a piece unmistakably a work of Georg Wojciechowski. You are taking a stand on the root soul of your music and saying to the world, 'this is what I believe in.' "

"I see. But 'prelude,' does that not mean 'something that comes before?' "

"Yes. I am stating that in which I believe, musically, in this opus of small pieces, now get ready for something really big coming next in the same way."

"What is your big thing coming next?"

"You always go for the roundhouse right hook, don't you Lin Xin Qian?"

"That is a boxing idiom, I believe. Yes why not go for the knockout? What do your preludes prepare us for?"

Georg stopped them on the path so they could turn face to face. The faintest sign of their breath condensing in the cool air confirmed summer approaching an end. Georg pushed out his answer without blinking.

"Grand opera."

They resumed their walk in the distinct, fast-paced New York tradition, deterring all interruption from outside.

Georg marched along silent and grim. Lin glanced over at him as if to inquire if more explanation were forthcoming. She chose not to say a word. But suddenly she took on a mischievous mood.

"Do you ever play the piano naked?"

"Off-balance! Nice one, Miss Xin."

"Do you?" she insisted, smiling broadly.

"You know I do."

"Yes."

Careening up the Henry Hudson Parkway in a taxi propelled onward by an aggressive driver with brilliant reaction skills, Georg and Lin headed for the Bronx. Lin curled up in her familiar style and thus faced Georg. They were consumed by a fast-paced discussion. Sometimes their bouncing comebacks overlapped.

"... well which is it, more dishes or ideograms?" he asked.

"I cannot answer until I know if you understand the writing system at all."

"The only thing I know is that the ideogram for 'Lin' looks like two trees and symbolizes a forest. But I still want to know, do you have more dishes in your cooking or ideograms in your writing?"

"Well, you like French food. How many dishes?"

"You are changing the subject and anyway I've talked with Lydia so many times about French cuisine and we've eaten a hundred French meals together and of course there is no given number, no total, you can't count all the variations and even then—"

"Evading."

"—you'd have to ask if one chef makes *Blanquette de Veau* the same any two times and so where does it become a separate 'dish'—"

"Evading."

"—but one thing she has told me on many occasions is that the Chinese chefs have such an exaggerated concept of their cuisine, that they think it is descended from the gods or something, and every other—"

"Wait, Chinese chefs have this attitude? I suppose French chefs are humble?"

"—and every other cuisine is like a can of soup compared to theirs. Once she made a joke, 'The hubris of the Chinese chef is vast and long, like the wall.' "

"Very funny."

Georg shifted forward to speak with the driver.

"Just past the Triborough you have to get off for the Third Street Bridge. You'll have to go down a ways across the river and come back, the place is actually practically under the bridge."

Only a grunt from the front seat acknowledged receipt of this information.

"You should not have this fight with me, I will be on top."

Georg fell back in his seat, slightly stunned and ignited.

"What, because of a Ten Thousand Year Banquet?"

"Yes."

"The kitchen of the Chrysanthemum Throne?"

"No, that is in Japan."

"Well in any case where does the flowery metaphor end, you don't want me to call that bluff, do you?"

"We will have the metaphor and you are defeated on that basis alone, but the reality is even better."

"Okay, okay, let me put this to you a different way."

"Go ahead, Monsieur Escargot."

"The bragging about the 47,000 ideograms?"

"The reality of the 47,000 ideograms."

"I happen to have read that to be considered literate, the number is 2,000."

"That is because you have a benchmark of literacy in English based on 'See Spot Run.' "

"How do you know about Spot?"

"Really miserable class in English as a Second Language."

This resulted in Georg laughing out loud with glowing eyes.

"Okay, okay, how about a master dish that is exquisite and unforgettable, with 47,000 ingredients?"

"Which dish?"

"*Bouillabaisse.* It has 47,000 different kinds of fish in it. Damn is that good, I had the real thing in Marseilles once and I never wanted to leave that table."

Lin did not blink. She remained stone faced, holding his gaze. After a dramatic interval she put on her loud and scary high-Mandarin priestess voice …

"Fuo Tiao Qiang."

Georg jerked back. His eyes went wide. He was rendered speechless. Lin struck while her adversary was stunned:

"Buddha Jumps Over The Wall!"

Deep in the labyrinthine workroom annex of Mozart Pianos, one instrument occupied a small room of its own. In the final stages of rebuild, it had not been touched for two weeks to allow certain glued elements to cure. It had not been touched in twenty years by an artist who could make it speak. The piano had been rescued from near oblivion.

The lid stood propped open, the brass inside shining brilliantly, polished now for the first time in decades. A row of clerestory windows let in bright rays of the sun, made visible by dust floating over and around the magnificent nine-foot black cabinet. Except for drifting clouds of this dust set in motion by eddies of late summer breezes leaking through old windows, nothing had disturbed this tableau for many days. Utter silence prevailed.

Now, faintly, voices. The sound of them gradually increased, several pairs of voices, engaging back and forth while walking fast. Dramatically, the group burst through the door and went silent at the sight. After a split-second pause, one man marched to the piano, sat imperiously and launched into thunderous music. Both his huge hands flew up and down the keys, moving so quickly as to blur the vision of those watching. The room barely contained the sound. Its walls focused it, sending it concentrated to the listeners who reacted as if struck by blows from a harmonious madman. For several minutes the piece roared on, with an embedded melody struggling to emerge from the center of the storm. When it did, it pierced with its beauty.

Nearing the end, the intensity of the pianist's physical prowess and precision increased, if possible, and the music closed with two giant chords that seemed to pin everything down.

The pianist got up fast and marched out a side door of the workroom, obviously intent on his next focus. All the others but two followed.

One of the remaining, a workman in a smock who over one month had painstakingly rebuilt the intricate action of the instrument, edged slowly to the keyboard, staring down at it. In a moment he raised his eyes to the other, an Asian-looking women, who was watching him with arms folded about her. They exchanged only a glance; no words were necessary. In his eyes shone incredulity, overmatched by awed delight. After a moment both walked off the way the others had departed, closing the door behind.

All voices and sounds ceased. The piano stood alone. Only storms of dust swept up into clouds by the violent blows of hammers on strings paid it tribute, as if delirious applause.

♦ Chopin, *Etude in C Minor,* op. 25 no. 12 ♦

Near the office inside the factory Georg brandished a list with the serial number of many pianos on it, seven of which had been checked off. He was just finishing a conversation with the owner as Lin approached. She had been wandering about the workshop.

"Well, I have a list of seven pianos here. Let me tell you the situation."

"Okay. Was that one you just played one of them?"

"No, that was a forty-year old Bösendorfer being restored. He just wanted me to play it so he and I could evaluate it. Can't be for the Piano Project, they are going to price it at about seventy-five thousand dollars."

"Holy cow!"

"Lin, mine is worth over a hundred and thirty-five thousand."

"I see."

"This project, here's how it works. I'm working two sides of the street here, I'm bringing volume cash business to Mozart Pianos because I have funding, not my own, from a benefactor, a music lover who contributes. So, I try to get as much money in my pool as possible, and I try to get the lowest possible price here. It can't be zero because the factory has costs already sunk into them. As I said, we take the better of the uprights, but ones that hardly anyone wants anymore; they are perfect for new pianists. My job is to check out the pianos, strike the price, make a purchase, then we find the pianos homes."

"Kids?"

"Yes. I'm involved with the young pianists. Sometimes I visit them, more often I call them. We have others who deal with the moving, tuning, providing lessons, etcetera."

"Georg, what was that music? I can still feel it in my lower back."

"Chopin, *Etude in C Minor,* opus 25 no. 12. It's even better on my piano in the middle of the night with *Château Margaux.*"

"Oh." He saw a shiver run through her body.

"Can you hold okay while I check these pianos? We can be gone in about half an hour, because we won't be negotiating today; I have three-day first refusal on them."

"It is nothing. This place is fascinating. But also, my presentation …"

"Yes?"

"This morning before I came up for breakfast, I awoke very early, I ran through the outline. I will think about it while you do this checking of pianos."

She shifted intensity. "It looks different to me now. I feel as light as a feather, but also … I have become very dangerous."

There was a moment between them. In all ways, in all emotions, and except for the touching of lips, they kissed.

From the terrace atop Georg's building the apartment showed few lights. A solitary figure cut a line through the long narrow pool: Lin swimming laps. Just enough illumination around the pool let her be observed, up and back. She wore the black one-piece swimsuit. Her strokes flailed in agitation, the water roiling as she thrust it out of the way.

Suddenly she stopped in mid-stroke and mid-lap to stand upright, motionless. The water churning around her hips subsided. Abruptly she reached for the lip of the pool, lifted herself out and without drying ran straight into the warm interior, making for the bar area. Water streamed off her body onto its tiled floor. She did not seem to care.

Lin opened the door of the refrigerator to retrieve a ripe mango. Finding a cutting board and knife, she attacked the fruit, peeling it longitudinally with the knife. Although the salon around her lay in darkness, one fixture made a pool of light precisely where she was working. Drops on her wet skin and the juicy mango glistened.

Halfway through the task she slowed. Each gesture became that of an aching, a longing for taste, piercing. She held half the mango and carefully sliced it into long pieces, arranging them in a fan on a beautiful porcelain plate. Now covered with juice, her hands completed each motion with expressiveness, something also found in her face, intent on opening the fruit yet inflected with roused sensation.

She reached for the second half of the mango. It slipped into her hand, slowly, lusciously. All motion stopped. Then, with obsession, she lifted her hand to her face to inhale the scent of the ripe fruit. She inhaled again, with increasing abandon. Her mouth took on a glisten where the wet fruit touched it.

Georg stood at the piano in the dark with headphones around his neck, staring at Lin, fixed on her since the moment she rose from the pool. With as much hunger as for his art, desire surged up his spine, exploding in his chest and throat, behind his eyes turning white hot. He threw off the headphones and ran across the room.

The quiet of deep night saturated the bedroom. Georg moved in the darkness, approaching the bed with just enough light to see sheets thrown back to reveal it empty. Then he heard the striking of a match from the other side of the large bedroom suite. A bloom of illumination blossomed behind a glass brick partition separating the bedroom from the art gallery.

As Georg walked around this wall a delightful scene greeted him. At the left side of an open stretch of floor a votive candle cast a pool of light where it rested on the hardwood. Its power prevailed there, but it did not effectively light the walls hung with glorious paintings, distant as they were.

Several feet to the right stood Lin, naked. The candlelight revealed her with its soft glow, but being the only illumination cast stark shadows behind her hip. Her arms rested at her side. She had pulled the black hair into a ponytail, leaving her face fully revealed, bare of makeup.

Georg approached slowly. She tracked him unblinkingly. He stopped ten feet from her.

"It is wonderful in bed with you," she said.

"It is?"

"Wonderful."

"It's easy, Lin. You're not afraid to be naked," he responded.

"How naked am I?"

"Turn to the right a little."

She moved slowly, holding his eyes with hers. He took his eyes away and made a feast with them of her nude body in the light coming from below, from the candle.

"Your belly is naked."

"Yes."

"And right there, the hollow in your hip."

She smiled at this description of her geography.

"The other one, too," she suggested.

"Let me see that."

She changed direction and came about until her other flank was fully illuminated. Sure enough, this hip was completely bare as well.

"Face away."

She rotated. The low light was particularly suited for this new prospect. With feet together she lifted off the floor onto tiptoes, causing muscles to define beneath the calves and smooth uppers of her legs. Her bottom rounded. The balancing act caused ripples beneath the skin of her back. She lifted an inch higher to make all these elements articulate to their fullest, then lowered the heels of her feet back to the floor.

"How light you are in your body. It was the first thing that called you to my attention."

"I love that phrase," she said, looking over her shoulder. "Your body called itself to my attention too."

"It did?"

"Right there in Lincoln Center. I wanted to see it with no clothes on immediately."

Georg delighted in this, gesturing to her, "A quarter around."

As she turned, maximum curvature was afforded. She shifted slightly to make a new pose, lifting her arms and stretching so breasts rose and back arched. She went up on tiptoes again to enlarge the effect.

"Around to front."

Lowering, she turned to face him. He walked over to her. Her eyes were shining.

"Very naked."

She nodded.

"One night as lovers, and you can be like this," he said.

"I like it."

"So do I."

"I like being naked. You can look at me as long as you want."

"Do you remember that modesty conversation we had yesterday walking through the park?" he asked.

"Oh yes. Right after you would not tell me anything about your grand opera and before we started fighting over cuisine."

"This is the result," he asserted.

"Yes. Modesty protected with the spirit of a warrior in the world, to be naked with as much strength and pride over again in private, when a lover's gift."

"Like this."

"Like this."

"It's better than I expected. It is magnificent."

"Do you know why you are wonderful in love-making?" she asked.

"No."

"How willing you are to have me completely naked. Many men would not be."

"It's true. Completely. I want it."

She hopped off her position and laughed a little, then began to step, strolling around him.

"Good thing. It would have been awkward to put everything back on." She whispered this close to his ear as she slipped past. She was not content merely to look; her hands touched as she circled. Georg surrendered to the caresses, making no counters. She executed a little dance move, then spun back to stand nearly as before. Her eyes and hands had taken full delight in Georg's nude body. Then she looked at him soberly.

"Especially once, before, when I was on top."

"Yes, that moment would be hard to take back."

"You were inside me, deep inside," she whispered.

"Yes, right then. You let me see everything."

"Yes I let you. That is when I was most naked."

Lin shook visibly, yet with strength in her face so monolithic to prove certain she would not back down from this moment. Georg moved within arm's reach. He was tried by emotion as well, and as well would not falter.

Lin's hand lifted to his face and touched his mouth. They could not speak, only adore each other with their eyes. Within, they discovered small sweet pools filled with risk and timelessness both. In these they stood awash, until by seeming magic their bodies floated to the bed again, entangled again, exulted again, slept.

Sunday

Georg and Lin celebrated Sunday morning in bed. They sat facing each other, smiling mischievously each time the thought of them became too rich. Lin kept an arm wrapped around her knees. They consumed red bananas and tangerines. Scattered and disarrayed sections of the New York Times littered the bed and floor. After a beautiful silence, Lin spoke.

"It is tomorrow in China."

"This is tomorrow."

"Are we still boyfriend-girlfriend?"

"Now I know you did not learn that in English as a Second Language."

"Television."

"We have a custom in America on the morning after a boy and a girl ... become friends."

"In China the father deploys a pitchfork if he finds them in bed. Tell me the American custom."

"If the party of the second part maintains sustained presence in the domicile of the party of the first part past ten a.m. he-she is considered to have made a tender of relationship."

"How awful."

"If subsequently the party of the first part proffers breakfast to the party of the second part and it is freely accepted, this in turn constitutes acquiescence and a legal and binding contract is deemed to have been created."

"Wait, they only have to have sex one night to get relationshipped?"

"And stay for breakfast, yes. That is correct. And what time is it and what meal are you eating?"

"You have no case whatsoever. This banana is substandard to qualify as breakfast. It is a snack. And since it is tomorrow, I have not acquiesced, consented or contracted in any way."

"First, that jape about—"

"You have been doing the Times crossword."

"Jape."

"That is a crossword word."

"—that jest about it being 'tomorrow' was Chinese flowery language again, inadmissible in this court. Today is this morning."

"I object! And anyway what about this little tiny weenie banana?"

"That is a personal slur, unmistakable. And these are red bananas, full grown and entirely precious. They are gorgeous."

"This information was not disclosed to me before my indictment."

"Your arguments are moot, since upon eating at least two of them ..."

"Three."

"... three of them, this erected a milepost in the case which ..."

"Erected a milepost? Erected? Poisoning the jury, coarsening the intercourse."

"We believe you to be out of order, far out of order."

"Who is we, did you bring me my next boyfriend? What kind of bananas does he have?"

Late in the afternoon, after several renewed efforts to explore the boy-girl entanglement through non-verbal means, the urge to venture out into the streets grabbed them. To do together. Be together. Be lovers in the city.

Lin having experienced New York twice previous to this current visit knew a place in Greenwich Village with which he was unfamiliar. She described a salmon crêpe with sauce velouté and a fine small hen with cognac in the stuffing. It had been nearly three years and they mutually pleaded with the cuisine gods that this restaurant remain alive and fine. They cast that fate to the wind, refusing to phone ahead.

In the cab down Seventh Avenue they exchanged a glance of inquiry as it went racing through the Theater District; then a mutual shake of the head over that idea. They sat close the rest of the way down, hips touching, silent, until deposited in Sheridan Square.

"We must walk," Lin said.

"You must have been to Europe," he said as they ventured up 4th Street.

"Yes, France and England. Also Italy," she replied.

"Me too, there's a lot to like."

"The Village has that feeling. This walking around and feeling happy about the shops and café life. They stay open, even on Sunday evening."

They came upon an artisan shop of flowers, the passion project of a sensitive proprietor resplendent in her bliss, beautiful. Lin and Georg spoke the names of varieties in whispers. They discovered some exotic ones, new to them, here and there. She turned to look seriously into his eyes.

"You have none in your salon," she remarked.

"No."

"You must. Right now. I am buying for you."

His objections died before escaping his lips. Even if only to accept in order to experience the yielding itself, frankly erotic, to see the deepening in her eyes when "Yes, okay" he said. She engaged the owner. He must surrender further, he discovered, when asked the sentiment the arrangement must speak. With a gesture Georg stopped Lin from offering anything. It took a moment, expectation building in the corner of the shop. Then it just fell out of him.

"We are new."

This was understood at once. Together, with the deft assistance of the floral artist, they assembled an array both jubilant and striking, yet delicate. Lin selected a vase and arranged delivery. She elicited the phone number to the lobby of their building and had the shop call ahead to notify the doorman to expect and hold the bouquet this evening.

Circling back around a block or two, headed for their dinner destination, the warmth from having received the caring gesture in the flowers would not, could not, be hidden; it told in his gait, his affections in touching, in his face. This day of everything had rendered him unguarded. She made no attempt to hide pleasure in having given this. As delicate as fragile blooms, translucent simple joys when taken up by warrior spirits.

Outside the restaurant he stopped her. The scent of wonderful things poured out when two happy diners exited and strode past them.

"I also like it, a lot, when you are ferocious," he said.

"I know."

"But not necessarily now, tonight."

"I am tender from the escape of so much rage, still."

"May I offer food and wine for that?" he said, delighted to think of it as a healing of her.

"Yes, this is the exact place."

They strolled in, arm in arm.

Monday

On Monday Lin vanished from the high salon into the business world of New York City. She reconnected with her team and together they pushed along the myriad details of her stupendous billion-plus capital transaction with Henry Lane's investment bank. While she and Lane did not meet in person, two intense phone conferences between them advanced things powerfully. All day long Lin's people shot spreadsheets and contract addenda back and forth with Lane's.

Her team did not pick up any signs of change in their boss. If some evidence slipped past her game face, she cancelled it out by stern focus and command.

In the early afternoon she sent them all out of her office on a mission and picked up the phone.

"Hello?"

"What key are you demolishing today, sir?" she asked with no preamble.

"E Flat. However it is impervious."

"Come on."

"No, really. Beethoven stands guard over it."

"I thought he demolished things."

"It does seem like he wants to smash things, but that is just his rage. He went deaf."

"Yes."

"This man went deaf."

"Yes."

"But I can hear fine. Say something."

"The taste of your mouth will not go away."

"I heard that. I hear it. Come get some more."

"Another three hours," she said.

"Hurry."

They hung up.

Georg and Lin luxuriated in the spa looking over Central Park. No noisy jets of water disturbed them, as they liked to talk in the water. It was quite hot, however. Also they kept touching and teasing, with a sumptuous kiss or two thrown in.

"I'm interested in the meaning of Machu Picchu," said Georg out of the blue.

"The meaning?"

"Well, what is it, a summer palace for a dictator? A religious retreat? An astronomical observatory? A 'last-stand' fortress? No one really knows."

"The Spanish never found it or sacked it, right?"

"Right. Well, I have a hypothesis about it."

"What?"

"There was a certain contingent of the Incas. They were born directly into objectivity. They had no concept of 'the afterlife.' No concept of 'the gods of everything.' No supernatural realm. Only ..." He spread his arms in a gesture of ostensible declaration of objective reality.

"I see," she said.

"They had to remove themselves. Everywhere else it was superstition, belief in gods and spirits, and especially attempting to control reality by magical incantation. And what this contingent really couldn't take, the thing that revolted them the most?"

"What?"

"Trying to gain value by destroying value, through sacrifice."

"Iye."

"The thing with sacrifice, to get the mojo working, to

make 'big medicine', the invisible god has to be as remote and potent as possible, and the thing you are sacrificing, killing, has to be more and more valuable and you must show yourself to be as helpless and impotent as possible. Supplication."

"You are right!"

"Otherwise, the sacrifice is 'not big enough,' and your god 'not mighty enough,' for instance to control the sun and the rain. This group had to get away from that insanity. They only believed in objective reality."

"I don't know. It seems whacky. What evidence do you have for this?"

"Whacky?"

"Whacky."

"Okay then. Well, the first thing I checked was, was there any evidence to the contrary. See, the default position of contemporary scholars is that every civilization is rooted in religion, superstition. This presupposition is so strong. It's really strong."

"Everyone assumes if it is an ancient culture, it is religious?" Lin posed.

"That's right. No thinkers even entertain the idea of objectivity. The default is, there's going to be religion. The social archeologists are sure of it. But at Machu Picchu they have no dominating building or temple or pyramid or anything, and especially no place clearly set aside for human sacrifice."

"Hmm."

"There are a few small 'places of importance' which naturally get called 'temples,' with interesting structures in them, but they seem to be astronomical, I mean factually astronomical, aligned to track the sun and stars. The main one is an object called the *Intihuatana*. So, because of the assumption of mystical religion right down to today, no one jumps to the possibility it was a civilization of rationals. They just say, well we have not figured out where the religion is, yet."

"We can't find the churches!" she joked.

"Yes. There is some evidence that there was a non-supernatural streak in the Incas, that they were thoroughly Pagan, at least that they 'worshiped' reality itself, with awe. One Inca told the Spanish, 'The Christ that you speak of died, the Sun and Moon never die, besides how do you know your God created the world?' My idea is, the number of rationals was small. This leader or king, Amaru, was one. He couldn't force his belief system on the entire Inca Empire, millions were rabid with superstition. The Empire was glued together using it, combined with force.

"So, he built this retreat, which most people call a 're-ligious retreat.' I say, it was a refuge, yes, but also a deprogramming camp, where anyone showing the signs of doubting the monolithic paradigm of Inca beliefs would be brought, to live with rationals and to wash away religion."

"What is the point? Georg, no one is going to buy this. It is a fantasy."

"That's okay. But since there is no factual wrecking my idea, it's perfect for positing a rational culture, just for the pleasure of the outrage, just to float it as true, even if it didn't happen to be true in actuality."

"Wow. So—"

"Even if it did not happen at Machu Picchu, it could and would – and should – happen many other times in this world. See, in my mind some people are born into objective reality and never swallow mystical beliefs, ever. No matter what the culture. This could have happened, in more than one place."

"I see. You could use it to stir up trouble at a party or something. Or to show people's prejudice that the irrational is the default."

Georg stared at her intensely for a long moment.

"I'm writing an opera with this as the plot."

"Holy shit."

He continued to stare. Lin absorbed it, then worked her way back around to the picture of it in her mind.

"Holy shit."

Georg laughed out loud. "It's so hilarious to see this serene Chinese face and big eyes, then you swear like a British truck driver."

"Holy *fucking* shit."

He laughed again. She was a spitfire.

"You are really writing it?"

He nodded slowly.

"They are completely rational?"

"Yes."

"It is not a slave city?"

"No."

"No human sacrifice?"

"No."

"No shamans?"

"No."

Lin looked up at him slowly.

"They have scientists?"

"Beginning ones. The *Intihuatana* is astronomical, not mystical."

"This is your grand opera."

"Yes."

There followed a long exchange of glances and much emotion. Lin's focus extended far off, imagining. In a low voice, she finally spoke, in simple honesty and admiration, nodding.

"You made the hair stand up on the back of my neck."

They climbed out of the hot water. Then a long sequence of towels, robes, a drink of water, eye contact, thinking; she was silent in awe of the idea. Once again he watched with open pleasure as she dried her long hair. Finally she spoke.

"When can I hear the arias?"

"Amaru's, very soon."

Tuesday

Tuesday morning Lin and Georg managed to take breakfast together before she ran out to her office in Manhattan.

"You have me spinning," she said.

"Really?"

"Yes, last night, the part about some people, anywhere, anytime, being born into objectivity and they are impervious to programming. They never lose sight of reality. They only go by their own judgment. That idea has me spinning."

"One reason I wanted to set the story back in time and in a seemingly monolithic shoebox was to make Amaru's natural objectivity and individualism stand out starkly. In today's world it's not completely monolithic; luckily, millions of children escape religious indoctrination."

"Our communism forbade it."

"Yes, ironically."

"You are going to say 'Yes, religious programming forbidden, but at the cost of indoctrination into political collectivism, to be a comrade.' "

"Yes," he affirmed.

"I am with you. It is an awful price."

"Lin, I have to take something back I just said."

"What?"

"Yes, it's true millions of children escape religious indoctrination today, but think of all the ones who do not escape it."

"Parents indoctrinate them."

"Yes, but worse, whole cultures, including government, are set up to make it happen. The authorities teach the parents to do it, force them to do it, or take over the job themselves."

"Oh."

"Muslim radical cultures."

"Yes."

"We're already a year into the twenty-first century. Why is it growing, I can't understand it."

"They are scary," she said.

"You can be executed or put in prison for simply rejecting the faith into which you are born. Today."

" 'Apostasy,' that is the word?"

"Yes. They push fear of hellfire and lust for heaven to such an extent it becomes politically real. You must hate and refuse the secular world. Some of them preach that young people must take violent action to destroy it."

Lin considered him carefully. Seeing Georg become agitated, tapping one foot on the kitchen floor and frowning deeply, her focus shifted from awareness of this topic as general discussion to something personal.

"The Christians used to be like that, before the Enlightenment."

His head snapped up to look at her. She remained stoic.

"They scared people into obeying," she continued, "tortured people, started wars and used the entire culture to indoctrinate children. And executed."

For seconds Georg locked eyes with her, jaw tightening, eyes turning dark. She did not react, merely supported whatever was roiling through him. Then he let go a little and sank back in his chair. He said only one thing more on the subject.

"Yes, I know."

The Tuesday night dinner party for Mark reached dessert. Many wine glasses stood on the table with Georg in the process of adding a champagne flute to each place. The table was set to accommodate six with only five present, Georg and Lin, Mark and Lauren and Professor Benjamin Soebel. In a place of prominence on a sideboard of the dining room the glorious arrangement of flowers dazzled with its subtle colors.

The guests babbled along. Georg seemed to be at the party but not exactly of it. Lin checked in with him now and then through affectionate touches and looks. At one point he drew her aside and whispered to her "Amaru has me stirred up." She nodded in understanding.

The doorman buzzer went off and Georg walked over to speak into the intercom. He returned to the table.

"That was her," Georg announced. "Your friend Angela, Benjamin. She's on her way up now."

"Good. I'm glad she made it for dessert at least," replied Benjamin. "Mark, she had a professional engagement she could not change and asked me to apologize to you. I forgot to do that earlier."

"No problem. You told her to bring me some cashmere from *Brunello Cucinelli* to make up for it, right?" With this quip Mark disappeared around the corner of the dining room.

"Lin, I hope you don't mind repeating your story about 'Buddha Jumps Over The Wall', maybe a short version," said Benjamin. "She'll really get a kick out of it."

"Not at all, Professor. I am tipsy from that Bordeaux, though; I might not remember all the ingredients." Benjamin and Lauren continued discussing the dish with Lin, arguing ridiculously and happily.

Angela arrived though the elevator vestibule entrance. As she moved into the dining room Georg and Benjamin saluted her with Puccini, overlapping in song.

"O soave fanciulla, o dolce vise di mite circonfuso alba lunar."

Angela halted in her tracks to absorb this tune directed at her from less than stellar operatic voices.

"Whoa that is quite a welcome. Who are you guys, the

punch-drunk gondoliers?"

"They've been doing that all night," said Lauren, "every time Lin or I come in the room. Mark taught them."

"O soave fanciulla, your name is Angela, right?" asked Georg.

"Yes and I've got to tell Mark I am really sorry I couldn't be here for this celebration dinner. Was it fun? Where is he?"

"Yes and only seven ingredients in the entire dinner."

Angela looked at Georg with an odd expression over this comment. Benjamin introduced her around the table. He seemed to be the only one who knew her.

"Well can't you get them to stop this dreadful singing? It must be Italian, what does it mean?" Angela said.

"No, we like it," said Lin. "We have gone out to the kitchen and back several times for no reason, just to get them to sing it. Unless Mark is lying to us, it means 'Oh, sweet beautiful maiden, oh, how your face looks, its beauty softly bathed by the gentle moonlight.' "

Everyone laughed.

"Oh very well! This is definitely wine-induced. But we should have a cracker-jack comeback for these guys, don't you think?"

"Yes, yes but what?" cried Lin. "Help us out. We can not think anymore due to wine. The best we could come up with was, 'Stop, in the Name of Love,' and that seems to be having no effect whatsoever."

"Well, let me see what I can do."

Mark walked back in the room having changed into a Paris poet's shirt. Angela put down her wine glass and began to walk slowly up one side of the large table. The others now noticed she wore a dress with embroidery of flowers. Seamlessly she transformed into Mimi. Mark set a music player he had been concealing on the table and turned it on; it contained the orchestral backing for the love duet from Puccini's opera *La Bohème*. He inhabited Rodolfo and walked up the other side of the table. The room was transported to Paris of 1846.

La Bohème

by Giacomo Puccini, Act 1 Love Duet

Rodolfo:
O soave fanciulla, o dolce viso
di mite circonfuso alba lunar,
in te ravviso il segno
ch'io vorrei sempre sognar!

Rodolfo:
Oh lovely girl, oh sweet face
bathed in the soft moonlight.
I see you in a dream
I'd dream forever!

**Rodolfo and Mimi sing together, different lyrics,
walking along opposite sides of the table.**

Rodolfo:
Fremon nell'anima
dolcezze este
Nel baccio freme amor
(Already I taste in spirit
the heights of tenderness!
Love trembles at our kiss!)

Mimi:
Oh come dolci scendono
le sue lusinghe al cur …
Tu sol commando, amor!
(How sweet his praises
enter my heart …
Love, you alone rule!)

**They arrive at the end of the table. Rodolfo attempts to
kiss her. Mimi turns her head away.**

Mimi: No, per pieta!
Rodolfo: Sei mia!
Mimi: V'aspettan gli amici …
Rodolfo: Già mi mandi via?
Mimi: Vorrei dir … ma non oso …
Rodolfo – (With gentility): Dì
Mimi: Se venissi con voi?
Rodolfo: Che? … Mimì?
    Sarebbe così dolce restar qui.
    C'è freddo fuori.
Mimi: Vi starò vicina! …
Rodolfo: E al ritorno?
Mimi: Curioso!
Rodolfo: Dammi il braccio, mia piccina.
Mimi: Obbedisco, signor!

Mimi: No, please!
Rodolfo: You're mine.
Mimi: Your friends are waiting.
Rodolfo: You send me away already?
Mimi: I dare not say what I'd like …
Rodolfo – (With gentility): Tell me.
Mimi: If I came with you … ?
Rodolfo: What? Mimi?
    It would be so fine to stay here..
    Outside it's cold.
Mimi: I'd be near you!
Rodolfo: And when we come back?
Mimi: We shall see!
Rodolfo: Give me your arm, my dear …
Mimi: Your servant, sir …

Arm in arm they begin to walk away

Rodolfo: Che m'ami di' …
Mimi: Io t'amo!

Rodolfo: Tell me you love me!
Mimi: I love you.

They walk out, their voices heard from offstage:

Rodolfo and Mimi:
Amor! Amor! Amor!

Rodolfo and Mimi:
Love! Love! Love!

At the end the lovers reached the top: double high C on a sustained, soft, piercing summit. When the last strains faded away, applause and 'bravos' rang out from the others. Mark and Angela took bows. She turned and curtseyed to Mark.

Lauren, above the cheers and exclamations, hands on hips, called out, "Wait a minute, wait a minute honey, step away from the tenor."

Much laughter ensued and Angela faked jealousy.

Lauren raised her voice: "I don't have the slightest clue what one word of that meant, but that was about *sex*."

Tremendous laughter and approval rained down. Georg and Benjamin set about opening the champagne and serving cake to all guests. Angela taught Lin and Lauren to make the characteristic gesture of an Italian woman turning away from a man's kiss and how to say 'No, per pieta!' when doing so. It was not lost on the three of them that this phrase included both 'no' and 'yes please' inside it. Eventually, all were ready to toast the guest of honor.

"Well, obviously Professor Soebel has brought in a ringer," said Georg. "Miss Angela, you are evidently a soprano, and with a beautiful 'C' I might add." She nodded a thank you to him. "And evidently there was a conspiracy afoot, very nicely done, Mark, you got us."

"I risked it," replied Mark, "but I told Angela on the phone we couldn't throw in a real kiss, like Alagna and Gheorghiu do. I'm not stupid, we are on the thirty-eighth floor."

"Damn straight," Lauren said, to general laughter.

"Mark and I spent the afternoon together today working on my big aria, his big aria. He gave a lot." Then Georg shifted to announcement mode. "A few days ago, Mark pushed me to let him sing this thing at his two big auditions, Saturday in Boston and next week in Los Angeles. I'm glad he pushed for it. It really shows off his voice."

"It's a show stopper," threw in Mark.

"Mark, we all are pulling for you like mad, we want to see your name higher and higher on the playbill all the time. You've worked everything so well to get in this position, now go get 'em. Make the hair stand up on Bucchi's head. Salute."

All joined in the toast of general praise and encouragement for Mark. They asked him for a few details about his dates and prospects, including the exciting possibility of him singing Marcello in Los Angeles. In the hubbub and crosstalk Mark was heard to make his sardonic joke again about joining the company of City Opera of Los Angeles and renting a condo in Santa Monica in order to get a tan.

Gradually, conversation wound down. Everyone looked at Mark, who was babbling on. No one moved.

"What?" he asked.

No one said anything at first.

"What?"

"We want to hear it," said Benjamin.

Sobering, Mark glanced at Georg, who nodded. Mark looked around the table at each guest, then stood without a word and exited the dining room.

"He's already in character. Come on, everyone," said Georg.

Georg led them out of the dining room toward the salon area, walking ahead of the others to open the curtains. Gasps erupted from the guests when the lights of New York erupted all around, especially Angela who had never been in the penthouse. They spotted Mark out on the deck, his normal shirt back on.

"Amaru is the son of a king, a king who is in conquest mode," began Georg. "Amaru does not fit in. He is a man of peace and learning. He does not agree with the religious orthodoxy. In this scene he has just heard his love, Quilla, singing about the night and the stars and the joy of being alive. He pours out his feelings about the exact same things but with pain and determination not to partake in conquest or superstition. He lives in primitive times but longs for true civilization."

Georg sat at the keyboard and began to play the low bass theme that forms the aria's background. Mark heard this and came in through a sliding door. In character, he took a position near the piano and sang the aria, which ended on a tumultuous crescendo and a power high note.

Applause and acclaim filled the salon. There was discussion of who got goose bumps. The three woman gathered close to Mark and conducted a mock groupie moment, including squeals. Lin actually flashed him the key to her hotel room. Lauren pushed the other two away.

"All you can have is an autograph. He's going home with me, almost immediately."

"I felt that B in my chest," said Georg. "That's power."

Shaking hands with Georg, Mark told him, "I'm ready for more."

"I think you need to watch your voice, don't you? That was all out, and you put in a lot today."

"No, I mean I'm ready for the next scene – scenes – to become real now."

With a frown, Georg responded, "The opera is on hold, I'm working on *The Preludes* now."

"Why is it on hold?" asked Mark.

Lauren said, "Mark ..."

"Why is it on hold, Georg?" challenged Mark, calm but assertive.

"I want to know the answer to that too." All eyes swiveled to Benjamin. He had spoken with flat intent.

Georg turned back to Mark. "You have this massive aria for your two big auditions. I've promised to do everything I can to get you the lead in the first performance, the world premiere, anywhere, whenever that takes place."

"When will that be?" asked Benjamin, approaching the two men.

"When the time is right."

"I'm sorry, Georg, but I have something to tell you," continued Benjamin. "This is the moment. First, I am asking you right now to release me from the promise of silence on the opera, the promise to which you bound me three weeks ago. I need to tell these people everything. Second, I've already overstepped the boundary of that promise anyway; Mark already knows everything. He's been studying the entire score."

Mark interjected, "I already know you've figured out how to leave the lovers living and free at the end."

Lin and Lauren looked at each other, amazed. Mark and Benjamin were standing close to Georg, not hiding in any way; they held his glance, which traversed from one to the other.

"It is for the good of the opera. Will you tell them?" insisted Benjamin.

No matter how much good will in a push, it is still a push. No matter how right he is, it is still rude. In a deeper flash: the biggest resentment is over him shoving me before I do it to myself.

"The opera is finished," Georg said. "The name of it is *Amaru Youpanki*, which is the name of the hero. It has been finished for a month. That includes a three-day exhausting rework with Benjamin. I even have digital orchestra files for the entire piece."

"But no rehearsals with live singers, no plans for bringing it out, right?"

"No. There is nowhere to bring it out, no one to bring it out to. I am not wanted as a composer. Why did you go against me on this, Benjamin?"

Benjamin stepped close to Georg. Mark backed away.

"I couldn't stand it any longer seeing you isolated up here in this miserable artist's garret composing arias and preludes, when you should be traveling the world with your operas and piano concertos."

A gasp from Lin. The others were stunned silent.

"Fuck."

"That's right."

"It's my work."

"This opera should belong not to you, but to the world now."

"Fuck."

"I am not finished," said Benjamin, pressing his case. "I am going to prove what I just said, that this opera is so good it must be shown to the world. Mark knows everything about Amaru now. It is his part. You have no idea how tightly it has hold of him."

"I am walking around in his soul for hours every day now," Mark injected.

"But I have had one other person study just Act 2, Scene 2, Georg, and I want you to trust me now. Get out of the way for the moment and trust me. You need this perspective."

"You've got me in a hard place, sir."

"I know. But during the entire time of our rewrite, I never pressed you on bringing it out, did I?"

"No."

"Or in the three weeks since?"

"No."

"You can call me 'sir' if you wish, I understand. And Georg, you can halt this process if you wish. I am putting this back in your hands now. I may be bushwhacking you, but it *is* your work, of course."

Benjamin handed Georg a CD. "This is the full orchestration of the second part of Act 2, Scene 2. If you don't want to proceed, hand it back to me; I will never mention it again. If you want to get this opera in play, to get the buzz rolling starting with the key people in this room, put the CD in the sound system. Decide."

Georg held the eyes of his mentor for a long moment. Then he turned and walked to the control center of the sound system. As soon as he stirred, Benjamin signaled Lin and Lauren to step back. Angela had not moved a muscle in five minutes. She was standing next to Mark in front of the piano.

Benjamin spoke:

"Act 2, Scene 2, on the terrace of a retreat hut on a mountainside above the city of Machu Picchu. It is dawn. Amaru and Quilla have been making love all night. During the first part of the scene, they are talking as lovers and reveling in the return of the sun for another day, a transformed day. Now, however, Amaru tells her that they have to confront his father and indeed the priests and entire royal court.

"Their love is illegal according to the king's rules, for one thing, but moreover they must make an attempt to dissuade the king from his policy of conquest and exploitation. They sing of the risk, their high purpose and how their hearts burn with the realization that although they love each other with intensity great as the sun, they may die before the day is over."

The music began. It was a fully-realized orchestra render. Mark and Angela fell into character. They sang the duet against the powerful orchestra.

♦ Amaru/Quilla duet ♦

This time there was no applause. The silence endured, laden with respect. Angela and Mark were not surprised by this, or upset; they just stood in place, waiting.

Georg emerged from the corner. He wore an expression of defiance, the full measure of bitterness not shielded from his mentor.

"This will be assassinated just like my piano concerto two years ago," he said.

"Perhaps," responded Benjamin.

"Even if some people, not critics, like it."

"Perhaps."

"Nothing has changed. I am on the outside of music."

"You did not try hard enough two years ago, Georg," said Benjamin.

Georg's head snapped up. Someone gasped in the room.

"What?"

"You did not try hard enough."

"What am I supposed to do, use a gun?"

"You went into a shell when the critics unloaded. No one could talk to you. I tried. I fed you a few ideas, like that workshop and showcase for advanced students. Did you follow that up?"

Georg did not respond and that was his answer.

"You don't like small steps like that. Too humiliating?"

"Benjamin ..."

"This music is magnificent. Just as I said, you have to

give it to the world. That means doing whatever you have to do to get it heard. Bypass the critics and the establishment. You have to."

Mark stirred. "If you thought there was no chance, why do you keep composing?"

Georg looked at him. He could not say a thing. Everyone knew the answer.

"Georg."

All eyes shifted to Lin, who stood proud and unashamed of the tears on her face. With certitude, she faced him down.

"You will bring this opera to China."

Wednesday

Georg had the salon to himself all day Wednesday and into the evening. He took advantage and executed one of the most productive, intense and satisfying sessions of composing in his life. The shock treatment issued by his mentor he credited for contributing to the surge, specifically. That included once or twice during the day the exclamation "Thank you, Benjamin" thrown against the wall, even if no one was there to hear it. Now, however, his own tenacious will took control.

While toying with lunch he was gradually taken over by an idea and bolted out of the kitchen, chair falling over. Later, standing next to the piano working on it, frustrated and angry, he began to curse Benjamin. It was more of the same all day, heaving to and fro, yet with victory and safe harbor at the end.

Early in the day Georg phoned Angela before her departure to Los Angeles, which was her base city. This was his moment to move off his stuck position. He proposed a showcase for the opera *Amaru Youpanki*. Angela lit up with the idea immediately. Besides the connection with her, the choice of Los Angeles reflected his belief that the Los Angeles opera scene welcomed alternate ideas and that Mark was headed there and hoped to stay there. Mark was his committed passionate ambassador. At the end of the conversation Angela announced with dead certainty, "I am Quilla." He did not argue.

He finished the call with a smile, then progressed into the bedroom, pulling sheets off the bed, finding others freshly laundered at the ready. He slowly settled them in place, performing this task as if a ritual, a lover's ritual. As a clean luxurious top sheet settled onto the bed, a new melody emerged in his aural intelligence, sweet, luscious and erotic. He ran out of the bedroom and headed straight for the piano.

It was dark now. Georg raced through the music earlier thought to be an etude but which now had an orchestra behind it. Lin arrived, dressed in a cocktail dress. She pulled off a wrap she was wearing, draped it over the back of the sofa and curled up to listen to the music.

As it ended, on a rambunctious dazzle of sound, Georg jumped off the piano bench and turned to her with arms spread out wide, wearing a mischievous look that admitted he had been humorously trumped by his own creation.

"What *is* that?"

"I've been slaving over the piano concerto and preludes all day, then I decided to take a look at that etude I wrote Friday. Then this happened."

"It got big."

"Yes, gigantic. It's the new ending of the first movement of the concerto. I had to transpose the key to make it fit. The orchestra is playing the melody, not the piano. It meshes with other material in the first movement I've had in the can for quite a while, but I never could get the ending. Amazing."

"Just like that, a major work?"

"Yes. Also, a very interesting melody bloomed up earlier. It has fallen into the second movement."

"Interesting?"

"Sensual."

She stood up and wrapped herself in him. It was not a hug. He whispered in her ear.

"You are very attractive in this dress. Bare shoulders."

"You are very attractive in that piano concerto."

"Really, I could watch you move around in it for several hours. Others were watching tonight though. I don't like that. But don't take it off yet."

"I crave a shower and soft clothes and someone eager to hear my exploits."

"Done. But could we have a liqueur with your hair up and my fingers tugging at these little straps first?"

"And with you making additional declarations of possessing me, both over the line and right on the mark?"

"I am reckless with it. But I can play the piano to make up for my sins."

"You do know the effect of such music and being nearby the first time such sounds are heard and being close to the source … erer? On me? She placed her lips near his ear. "Arousal."

She moved out of his arms, tugged the dress into place, put a finger under one of the spaghetti straps, running it to the top of the shoulder in order to move it over just an inch. Then she spun around, walked away, swaying nicely, with one glance over her shoulder.

"I will fix something for us."

While Lin proceeded to pour, she began to run out her story.

"The presentation run-through was tremendous. I have a new sequence now. And during dinner with Henry Lane tonight, we threw in some provocative twists. He is radical."

"This was at The Four Seasons?"

"Yes."

"Can you summarize it for me?"

"You can sell by activating the customer's fears and insecurities, then provide a salve. Additionally, you can engineer products and services that only sell if the customer reaches higher, from within. I am teaching the core of this second approach. How to design the products and how to connect with the higher self of the customer."

"This must be a difficult sell."

"I put it in practical terms. There will be less and less wealth to extract through a gamed economy much longer.

Detroit, heavy industry, electronics, even banking, service and retail have suffered in the US. The US is failing in the marketplace. You worked up the ambition to become France and you are almost there."

"Everyone at this presentation will know about your enterprise in China?"

"Yes. So I have some credibility, as you might imagine. They will all be briefed on the exact reason Henry Lane is going forward with us, both on the level of this specific one point three billion dollar extremely profitable transaction and also on why my country's free market enterprise could save the world."

There was a significant pause. Georg looked in her face, waiting to see if she had a charge on her last statement.

"You could not have used that exact phrase a few days ago," he said softly. "My country."

"No."

"I think I understand a little better now."

"Georg, I still do not trust the Communists. I hate them more than ever. I hate that China is in chains to them. Nevertheless, at this moment we have conditions under which my family has always prospered. In this window, there is more freedom and capitalism in China than here. It is likely to last for a generation, perhaps two, so China can be modern. I am extremely cynical that it emanates from any sort of moral or philosophical base, so I will live with one foot out of the basket for the rest of my life."

"I see."

"But if I am going to do any good, I must operate out of *my* beliefs, my moral center. My rage had to be spoken."

"I have never witnessed courage like that. I was honored."

Lin came close to him. She extended her hand, palm up.

"I will tell you now the reason I wanted to be here, my off-balance reason. I knew immediately, beginning when you laughed at my cowboy joke and made your impossible money-is-enslaved statement, you are with me at this root. That stunned me. Then later I knew from the emotion in your preludes that if my rage exploded, you had the character to hold up under it as my witness."

"Lin—"

"And be my champion. No one else ever in my life, family, friends, not my uncle or sister could have been. Not my parents, much as I love them."

"How did you know—?"

"Not any of the men who have courted me in China."

Georg jolted to a stop. His heart turned. He accepted her judgment of him. He accepted the rightness of her choosing him.

"Georg, *I* was honored," she finished.

They held each other with their eyes. Neither quailed, neither hid.

After perfect moments, Lin stood up, offered her hand to him.

"Take a shower with me."

They began to walk to the bedroom. She put a finger under one of her dress straps and slid it off her shoulder so it fell down along her upper arm. He enjoyed that gesture significantly.

"Bare shoulders. Very pretty."

"Once I said I would tell you the meaning of 'Qian' if you ever said it in English?"

"Yes, does it mean 'bare shoulders'?"

"No, ridiculous person. It means 'pretty.' "

"Ha!"

"But I have to tell you, that is only when it is given as a name to a girl. 'Qian' in daytime use means 'money.' "

"No!"

"Uh-huh," she said, nodding.

They looked at each other with incredulity for a full second, then burst out laughing. The confluence was simply delicious. They needed no further words, only two or three waves of hilarity sweeping over them to cinch it down. They continued their walk into the bathroom.

"So, four days from tomorrow you are going to tell Lane's elite shock troops to abandon the benefits of being in a cartel with the government, start appealing to excellence in the hearts of Americans and to take a lesson on capitalism from the People's Republic of China?"

"Yes." Sliding off the other strap she held the dress up with a hand on her chest as she walked.

"You are going to rattle the bones."

Thursday

Mark and Georg met for lunch.

"… a piano concerto?"

"Yes, it is pouring out. Apparently my subconscious has been working on it for quite a while. Even the orchestration."

"In your all-out Romantic style, right?"

"Of course. Hell, if I'm being flushed out of my garret, I might as well be as foolish as possible. Otherwise, what's the point of having been reluctant all this time? I mean good foolish."

"I know. In case you haven't noticed, I am in the foolish boat with you."

"Uh-oh."

"Don't worry, I am not regretting, far from it. But I wish I had some better gallows humor about it."

"What's the best you have now?"

" 'They loved the young tenor's articulation and his meticulous avoidance of inappropriate portamento, but expressed regret that the composer of his chosen aria was unfortunately not a dead European person, but whom should be immediately shot for writing it.' "

"That's pretty damn good," said Georg. "How about 'We love your power in this high tessitura but don't you have something better than a dreadful tune from a dinner-theater melodrama? It's making us queasy!' "

"Okay, I just got another one," said Mark. "Your feelings won't be hurt?"

"Hit me with your best shot."

" 'What is that, Barry Manilow?' "

"I tell them, 'Zjedz moj chug.' "

"That's Polish for …?"

"Eat my dick."

Mark erupted, beside himself laughing. Other diners stared at their table when he almost fell off his chair.

"Georg, all kidding aside, there are several things you don't know and also we have to talk strategy. I have about two hours for this lunch, that's it. I have dinner and dancing with Lauren tonight. And other activities. Ever since that party, she's been on fire. She can't keep her shirt on for two minutes, she took it off going up in the elevator yesterday for Pete's sake, with nothing underneath, and she won't let me keep my pants on more than—"

"Too much information."

"Okay, okay, but I am the Inca fertility god these days and she is propitiating, let's leave it at that … Our plane leaves at nine a.m. tomorrow, I've got appointments in Boston at lunchtime after I arrive. She'll be with me for the weekend up there, but not out to Los Angeles Monday."

"What don't I know?"

"Well, Angela is back in LA now, of course. Actually, I am expecting her to call while we're sitting here. She liked your plan for a West Coast showcase so much, and oh by the way Quilla has gotten under her skin bad, she's put out a few feelers. We could have some actual development while I am out there on this audition. She's started up an invitee list for the showcase."

"Whoa, that's great. Can you drop any big names on me?"

"What makes you think she has any big names?"

"Come on …"

"Okay, okay. Georg, she believes she will be crossing paths with Alexander Corbin or at least with his people high up in City Opera of Los Angeles."

"You are going to cross paths with City Opera."

"But just for an audition. To get on the cast of *La Bo-*

hème as Marcello. I have no real relationship. Angela has a girlfriend who is an assistant to Corbin himself."

"So where will that get us?" asked Georg.

"We are joking about critics mocking Amaru's aria, but frankly, it is a singer's song. Corbin himself will love the showmanship in it. Corbin, a high tenor, a great one, is artistic director of COLA, that's astounding. Now, he would not normally appear at my entry-level audition. But if we can pass the word inside, perhaps feed him a CD through Angela's friend, maybe he will become fascinated. He might at least tell the City Opera staff people to not dismiss the aria, nor myself as the singer of it, when I audition."

"That could lead to points for you, and buzz and creditability for *Amaru* when we showcase," said Georg.

"He might send somebody to the showcase. He might screen the video tape of it you would produce."

Georg noticed Mark filling with emotion. He was proud and dignified but suffering.

"Mark—"

"Don't say anything sympathetic. This is my aria and my part. I am going to fight like a possessed person for it, be warned my beautiful friend."

"You are afraid it will get swept away from you."

"It is no joke that the classical music intelligentsia will pour vitriol all over you, Georg. This you have dreaded. But singers will adore you. Orchestra players. Audiences oh … my … god. And you know who else?"

"Who?"

"Small and medium companies just like City Opera of Los Angeles who keep getting requests from their season ticket holders for new operas with melody, heroes, love, sex and victory, and these companies might not care what the critics say as long as you, Georg Wojciechowski, can fill their house. You should go out there right away and showcase. You should send the tape of the showcase to every opera company in the world, large or small. You will get on the boards."

They held each other's glance with all the implications floating in the air over their lunch table. Mark's phone rang.

For a person who denounced a PDA for calendar, he was an early adaptor for mobile phone.

"Angela! Are you sitting under a palm tree? Well when I get there we are going to do exactly that, immediately. I hear there are lots of them at LAX and you know I have never seen one in person. What have you got for us? Georg is sitting right here with me."

Mark and Georg exited the restaurant after lunch.

"Not the greatest grilled sea bass ever …"

"My lamb was pretty good."

"Do we have everything straight?"

"Yes. Now go home and propitiate."

"Very funny. Lauren will want to, more than once. She can't go out to the coast with me Monday, she's doing some sort of backwoods mountain retreat or something."

"I'll stay close to the phone all day Saturday for your call," Georg said, "then at least we will have the reaction of two insiders. I hope you will be telling me that Bucchi and Carlisle are on your team and will put in a word for you with every opera company in existence. Really, if anything is right with the world, they have to crank up your legend."

"I like that, I like thinking of myself as a legend."

"You are taking a big chance throwing an unknown aria at an audition as important as this. My gratitude?" Georg made an expansive gesture and smiled, then turned serious. "I want this gamble to pay off for you."

"It will. I am legendary!" Mark paused and grew serious. "Lin is good for you, Georg. Are you in love with her?"

Georg did not say anything, merely offered his countenance to his friend, hiding nothing.

"This is the best worst trouble I want to see you in."

Mark paused, but Georg remained silent. Mark had one last thing to say.

"Thank you for Amaru."

Georg nodded to acknowledge. They shook hands. After one last glance, they walked their separate ways.

Lin found it necessary to extend her Thursday business

day into Thursday night, including a full run-through of all contract elements with her key people. Some details had only become finalized late in the day and she did not want to wait until Friday for the last full-scale examination of the deal. By the time she arrived on Central Park South her status combined two extremes: focus-effort exhaustion and exhilaration of a chase nearing climax.

She found Georg in nearly the same condition.

The evening passed in honor of the two emotions. They toasted each other with wine over a simple meal, expressions of regard expanding the thrill of strivers reaching high in all matters, as so did resting gently in each other's arms, wordlessly. A wonderful peace grew between them.

Late, they awoke. Neither knew who called the other from sleep first. Neither cared who lit carnal fires first with ecstatic kissing. Neither noticed the moment pass when one peak of pleasure turned exquisitely into ground for a steeper climb, reaching heights from which no descent seemed possible, nor ever wished be sought.

Friday

In the late afternoon Georg sat curled up on a sofa, Lin-fashion. Silence prevailed in the salon. Shortly, Lin arrived. Her business suit was sophisticated and elegant, but looked thoroughly done for the day. She set her briefcase down and moved slowly, detecting his mood. She landed on the sofa and waited.

"I can't stop laughing inside," he said.

"Laugh on the outside."

Obviously Lin was receptive. "It's been a ridiculous day. The piano music is flooding out. I'm laughing because it's so fast I can barely keep up with the ideas. My joke at one point was 'I need more RAM.' Mark is in Boston stirring things up, walking around in my character's soul. Angela in L.A. is under the spell of Quilla. She called me today to talk about Quilla's personality, and is conspiring on my behalf under the palms out there. I also spoke to Benjamin. He came over at once to listen to the concerto. He called me a son-of-a-bitch—"

"That is a swear word I like," Lin shot in.

"—and I laughed for ten minutes over that. I am being run ragged by my music libido. It's mainlining hormones into my bloodstream and taking over the joint. And then, any time my music arousal goes dormant for a second, I realize sexual heat is racing along underneath the whole time because my brain goes wild with images of what you are doing to me every night."

"Who me?"

"On top of that, Lydia calls from Florence today."

"Wow."

"As soon as I told her about *The Preludes* recital, the coming out of *Amaru Youpanki* and the concerto with Benjamin now furious to help me get it into an orchestra, she starts crying. Crying. Seventy dollars a minute on the phone from Florence, Italy, and she is crying for ten minutes, well that made me giddy all over again. You know what her punch line was?"

"What?"

" 'I just wanted to call to tell you how beautiful *The David* looks and now I wish I were in New York.' "

"You *are* a lucky son-of-a-bitch."

"Yes. She soon recovered her pragmatism, however. They are headed for Sienna tomorrow."

"What else?"

"Now that my friends have pulled me out into the sun, my pent-up drive is recklessly uncaring about being cautious."

"You walked out into the sun on your own."

"Yes. You are right, I take that back. Here's the biggest laugh of all: every situation I let hold me back? Now, I don't care anymore. But meanwhile, nothing is changed in the world. All my former apprehensions had a reason and the reasons are more true than ever. I am going to have to fight a war. But I don't care. This makes me so amused I am nauseous."

"Run them out. Get them out."

"I have the gall to write and perform ten preludes in the face of Chopin and Rachmaninoff and put myself in their seat. I don't care anymore, and the preludes are getting riskier all the time."

"That is a good one."

"Now a high-Romantic piano concerto is roaring down the track, with brass blaring and timpani thundering. I'm saying I am Grieg and Brahms and Tchaikovsky. Not to mention Sergei Rachmaninov. This piece cannot be performed except with a symphony orchestra in a concert setting, meanwhile the romance-bashers control the boards and this thing will make *them* nauseous. I don't care. I let Benjamin hear it and he is going berserk."

"You are sure to get crushed on that one."

"The opera. If anyone figures out the meaning of the opera, I will be worse than crushed."

"Explain."

"Okay, it is based on factual characters, the great Inka Pachakutiq who is their equivalent of Phillip, father of Alexander the Great. The glory, the high water mark of this culture. Yet, my hero, his son, says it is an immoral, superstitious, conquest culture. I am calling an indigenous culture hideous. Very politically incorrect. Second, the opera has plot, melody, chewing-the-scenery arias and a happy ending for the lovers. Very politically incorrect. Last, it attacks the entire idea of religion. It is not just anti-organized religion, it is anti-supernatural. Not even Gaia is safe around me. Very politically incorrect."

"I didn't know about that. Oh you are in serious trouble."

They stood up, spinning around each other, laughing. Lin threw off her suit jacket, revealing a splendid tailored blouse.

"I don't care, that is the amazing thing. I mean it. I don't care. I am ripping off Rach and Puccini, pandering to the old-school opera audience, insulting an indigenous pre-Columbian culture and blatantly shouting that prayer and sacrifice do not work. All kinds of crap is going to come down. But I don't care."

"You have become dangerous!"

"Yes! I don't even care that my cool has disappeared."

"Correct. You are naked and dangerous. Do not put your cool back on. It will diminish the charm for me."

"I am too far gone to put it back on. Now what the hell do you want to do tonight? It's Friday night, do you want to go out?"

"Yes! I want to get dressed up and go somewhere elegant. Feed me French food again. Take me dancing."

"Perfect. I'll make some calls. We are Grand Bourgeois? Make the most of it. We should spend at least five hundred dollars."

They started to walk to the bedroom, Lin unbuttoning her blouse.

"Take a shower with me."

"Xin-Xin, you are always saying that."

"And promise, after we come home we must make love. The authorities could arrest you for your musical crimes at any second."

Deep in the night Lin and Georg swam naked in opposite directions of the heated lap pool. They passed each other several times, sliding bodies together like dolphins courting. After one delicious encounter Georg reversed field to catch up with her. They stopped swimming to caress. His powerful hands on Lin's body sent shivers along her spine.

"This pool was designed for one person at a time," she said. "Or two not afraid to touch."

"We are not afraid of that," he said, arms encircling, drawing her body tight to his.

"I enjoyed pressing up against you while we were dancing. Did you notice it?"

"With the tips of your breasts?"

"Yes."

"Like now?"

"Yes."

"I was completely conscious of it every time, all night long."

"In this week together we have made love twelve times," Lin said gently.

"To me it seems continuous now, so I say 'only once.' "

"How many times do you have to make love to be in love?"

"Once."

Lin escaped his arms. She swam fast to the south end of the pool. Georg chased her, caught her. They embraced, standing in the water with New York all around. From high above Lin could be seen to escape again, climb out of the pool and reach her arm back to pull Georg out. Hand in hand, naked, they disappeared quickly inside.

Saturday

In the salon room morning Georg's hands raced up and down the keyboard executing dazzling exercises. Lin appeared in the background. She wore pajamas and a visage ruffled with sleep. She stared at him for a moment, hand on hip, then darted away.

The music sprinted on. She reappeared in the same spot with a big glass of orange juice. The music ceased; Georg spotted her.

"You don't have to stop," she said.

"I woke you."

"Yes so what. I made my bed, now I can not sleep in it."

He let out a big burst of laughter. "That was your best idiom joke yet."

"What time is it?"

"Ten-thirty."

"What day is it?"

"Saturday. Morning."

"Go ahead, go back to your damned *School of Velocity.* I need coffee."

Lin disappeared.

Georg ran down his Czerny for a while, until hunger caught up with him. In the kitchen he found Lin ineptly making toast and eggs. As she put down a plate on the table and turned away, he stole her seat and coffee. Lin grabbed his shirt and yanked him off the chair. Deeper into breakfast, both of them drank second cups of coffee out of big mugs, waving hands demonstrably; whatever it was, it was outrageous, funny and infuriating.

Later, during an oft aborted cleanup, the refrigerator door could be seen open. They were obviously kissing but only their legs below and tops of heads and hands and arms above the door were visible.

Lin in the shower, rinsing her hair. She stopped suddenly and turned her head looking for him. No one arrived in answer to her silent call. Georg stood next to the piano with headset on, conducting the overture to his opera. He loved it for a few moments, then threw up his hands in rejection, sat down at the computer and started typing furiously.

Lin, dressed now, with another mug of coffee, stood in the dining room with the presentation materials all around, her steely intensity as she studied the white board conveying the stakes of the project; presentation day was close at hand.

Around noon the two of them attempted to teach each other the cha-cha. They invented the steps as they cha'd along, as neither knew what they were doing. Abruptly, in the middle of an Enrique Jorrín classic, the phone rang. It was the call for which they had been waiting.

They both rushed to answer. Georg put it on speaker.

"Hello?"

"Georg."

"Mark, it's you. Lin is here too, what's up?"

"I am legendary."

Lin and Georg burst into happy shouting. When they subsided …

"I've been ringing their bells, baby."

"Mark this is so good. I mean, these guys are both conservatives you told me … What did they say?"

"I've got to talk fast. After the first aria, the tear

aria from *L'Elisir*, Bucchi made me do some scales and arpeggios, amazingly. Wanted to hear the deep detail of my voice, he said. Then he asked me to talk about how a pro would contend with 'Celeste Aida,' since it comes so early in the opera. Then Carlisle asks me to give a realistic assessment of my prospects. I told him I was ready for roles and expected to be booked in good ones across the nation, fast. That I'm a pro now. I gave him specifics. Then I said … I said I also had a rapid advancement plan."

Another exclamation from Lin and Georg.

"I said 'I believe you know I have a special aria for you. It's from an opera soon to be showcased on the West Coast.' They said they'd already decided to hear it out, wanted to know about this rapid advancement plan, though. I just said, 'I am going to ride this aria and this opera in the featured role at its world premiere, then travel with it to many houses over the next few years. That will make my career.' "

More whoops.

"Hell, their eyebrows went up, but they listened. Georg, I just went into character. I forgot they were there. Amaru loves this woman standing next to him, can have her, and yet risks everything. It's his line in the sand."

"Yes," said Georg.

"I was full of it, and had plenty left for the final B. A tenor knows when he has made the bell ring. I rang that fucking bell."

Lin put her arm through Georg's. Her eyes were wet.

"Oh Mark, Mark. You are going to be famous," she said.

"No one is taking this part away from me. Not Alexander Corbin, not even Placido Domingo, and he is going to want it."

"Congratulations, Mark."

"I have so much else to tell you, but I have to hang up in twenty seconds. I won't be able to call you back until tomorrow."

"Okay."

"But Georg, you have to do something. We'll discuss it

more in the morning, but you are being asked to overnight the full score and the full orchestra, and the takes we captured of Angela and me in the duet, one package out here and one to Boston. They have to arrive Tuesday morning. I don't have them."

"Who is asking?"

"Bucchi wants it …" Mark paused dramatically. "… and Angela's friend on Corbin's staff at City Opera Los Angeles, Amy Santos. Bucchi called her. We just got off the phone with Amy, that's why I am calling so late."

"Mark …"

"I've got to go, really. Just hold and be really happy and think about it overnight. Nothing more will happen until we call you. We'll call you in the morning, James Bucchi and I on conference. Be in your apartment until noon. And thank your stars you have a fucking legend singing your songs."

Mark hung up. Georg fell back deep in the sofa. They shared a long, exultant silence. Then Georg got up and walked to the windows that looked out over New York City. Lin followed. She simply stood at his side, waiting. In a moment, Georg calmly turned to look in her eyes.

"When do you return to China?"

"Wednesday."

Georg rocked back on his heels. It took many seconds before he could speak. "It never occurred to ask you before. In my dream world I assumed you would stay here forever. That is so blind. But just now it came over me: you are going back."

"Yes."

"How long have you known it would be that soon?"

"Just since yesterday. I spent an hour with my uncle on the phone. I have responsibilities with the new capital injection on the China end. I was going to tell you tonight."

A loaded calm came over Georg. His next words emerged gently.

"I'm in love with you Lin."

She held her face up to him, not moving. She held it there to let him see his sun shining in her eyes. Then she whispered, more gently than he.

"I am in love with you."

They did not touch, except with these eyes. These soft, warm eyes.

"I have to go to California now. Tomorrow. I may be out there for weeks, or more."

"Yes."

"You can't come with me …?"

Lin shook her head.

"You might come back to New York …?"

Lin did not move. Significantly, she only held his gaze, eyes now shiny and wet.

"I see." Then, he spoke simply.

"What's our count so far?"

"Fourteen."

Deep in the night Georg and Lin lay like spoons in the bed, wide awake. Only their bodies from the shoulders up emerged above the blankets.

"Georg?"

"Yes?"

"Where does your music come from?"

"I must look in your eyes for this."

Lin rotated in the bed.

"And your loving?" she added.

"You are up for discussing this like intellectuals?"

"Yes," Lin affirmed.

"Because we could discuss it the non-intellectual way. Again. Now."

"As so we have done in this bed. My appetite for such ways will come around again very soon."

"Okay then."

Georg paused. He enlarged the feeling of that which he was about to describe. Then he spoke.

"Sometimes I follow my thoughts to the end, to what exists. This building, feeling the root of it on a rock. Sometimes I lay in bed and feel it. This earth. We are clinging to the earth as it spins and whirls around the sun."

"Yes. I have done that too."

"Then the galaxy. Then millions of galaxies. If you slowly take it all into your awareness, the vast universe, stay sharp, stay focused, you will go into rapture.

"Then add one thing. There can be no such thing as a cause of it. If something had caused reality, it would have to first exist, and since the universe means 'everything that exists' then it could not 'cause existence.' So, there is no outside. There is no inside.

"The fact that there is no outside is not disturbing to me: it is thrilling. Or that notion 'Why is there something rather than nothing?' There is no such thing as nothing. There is no alternative! There is only existence. If you accept the finality of death, then the meaning you supply would be all the meaning there could be, and enough."

"Yes," she said.

"To face death as final. To be alive with no exit. Our thoughts, choices, actions … this is the meaning. The greater we make ourselves, the more life means."

"Yes."

"So, where does my love come from?"

"Yes, and the music, where?"

"The music, in the beauty of being alive, of choosing to be alive on this earth, here, now. It just jumps right out of that. The music is to celebrate existence without fear. To exalt in it."

Lin touched her lips with fingertips. "And the love in our touching?"

"You are not afraid to be naked in this world, Lin, as neither am I. You choose life in the face of death. So much courage. What you seek while alive, I seek. Xin-Xin we *make* love."

Lin brought her hands to her face, nearly overcome.

"How I do love you," she cried. "Alive and alone and filling up with you."

Sunday

At dawn Lin brought Georg awake with an attack on their dilemma. Characteristically, she launched into her pitch without preamble. He lay prone on the solid bed in the solid building rooted to the solid bedrock of Manhattan yet at first felt a sensation like vertigo, the disorientating effect he had come to sardonically call the 'Xin Unhinge.'

Then he joined her in the attack.

They did not win.

♦ The Battle in Bed, page 139 ♦

Lin sat at the table on the terrace. Remnants of Sunday brunch littered the place. She was unhappily reading a section of the paper. She looked across the table at Georg.

"The other day, when I said to you that the Christians used to be like the radical Muslims?"

"Yes?"

"You have something hurtful inside about that, do you not? I saw it in your face and you filled up with anger."

"Why are you bringing that up now?"

"I thought that day I should help you get it out. And there is a bad opinion piece here in the *Times* today about the radical Muslims. It reminded me."

"I would have wished that someday you would serve as my witness, Lin."

"As you did for me?"

"Yes. Lydia is fanatical about our family. It was she who urged us all not to Americanize our name. She has the family genealogy, some of it going back hundreds of years. We are a branch of the Potocki family. When my mother married Aleksy Wojciechowski that remained true, since he is also of that clan."

Georg paused to gather himself. "There were persecutions of my ancestors by Christians, Catholic authorities, and at least one burned alive for renouncing belief in god."

"Do you wish to talk about it now?"

"No. Not on our last day. State religion eats the same bones as Mao, Hitler and Stalin. Theocracy. Religion murdered through the religious Incas. It murdered my ancestors in Europe. It is still murdering. My anger will come to the surface when it must. I will make sure Amaru sings with my rage."

Georg's cordless phone rang. He began an animated back-and-forth, pacing on the terrace next to the pool.

"Okay ... that's perfect ... okay ... I think it's reasonable to meet by that time, we'll all be there and landed and everything tomorrow night ... okay. I will ... I had a fantastic meeting with Mark and James Bucchi on the phone this morning ... yes. Mark knows your friend Amy Santos now ... Angela, you are conducting yourself with professionalism, I want you to know that. I appreciate exactly that ... yes ... goodbye until Tuesday morning."

He signed off on the call and sat at the table.

"What can I say? This might still be complete spinning of wheels, a fool's errand, but it sure doesn't feel like it."

"Angela?"

"Yes. You know, she could produce this showcase, she's that organized and resourceful. But that won't happen. She needs to be the voice only, and pursue her other opportunities at the same time. I have to produce the showcase."

"So she will be singing Quilla?"

"I can't think why I would tamper with something already hot. They nailed that duet Tuesday night. Didn't you think so?"

"They thrilled me."

"I'll be flying to Los Angeles tomorrow afternoon. Mark also, from Boston. The two of us, plus Angela, Amy and one other person, a production assistant Angela likes, have a meeting Tuesday morning to plan the showcase for *Amaru Youpanki*."

"Mark in Los Angeles. That is fun to think about," laughed Lin.

"Mark is going to get anchored there, I bet. He will love it. His audition at City Opera of Los Angeles will go well. I am pretty sure he will at least get cast as understudy for Marcello in *La Bohème* and maybe he will win the part outright."

"What about Lauren? She is a New Yorker."

"Mark has a feeling about that. Let me put it this way. He related a daydream about shopping on Rodeo Drive and 'slipping into Van Cleef & Arpels.' Then he said something about retail highway robbery and mentioned he had heard of some place called 'Tustin Jewelry Exchange.' " Georg and Lin both shrugged in non-recognition. "Then he wouldn't talk about it anymore."

"Matrimony."

"You think so?"

"Not a pair of earrings, a ring. And Lauren will say 'yes.' You did not hear this the night of the party, Lauren said it to Angela and me, that when Mark gets around her she forgets all about her G-spot because he goes straight to her M-spot."

Georg laughed. "The M-spot is for marriage? Money?"

"Neither. For 'Mark.' Her Mark-spot. But Lauren will be happy to participate in matrimony and money, too. Do not worry about your friend, Lauren is a good person."

"I believe that. They are so young, though …" Georg said.

"Where is the money coming from for the showcase?" Lin asked, veering off.

"I have it."

"You son-of-a-bitch."

"This sounds like a cliché, but I earned it during my

twenties and invested and Lydia matched it, only on the condition it be used to mount a concert. I have forty thousand dollars."

"Son-of-a-bitch."

"The others don't know I have it, either. I am going to first be sure everyone is on board emotionally and in love with the piece, especially Amy, Alexander Corbin's assistant. When they start fretting about floating the budget, I'm going to slam my checkbook down on the table and tell them I have fifteen. That's plenty."

Lin just shook her head and smiled at him. Georg flushed with pride at his cool strategy.

"This must seem like play money and projects to you, Miss Billion," he said.

"Do not dare to start a fight."

"We have never had a fight. Marital bliss."

"Well, do not start now, we only have this afternoon before our divorce comes through."

"Oh."

"Georg, I have an intense day tomorrow. We are closing my billion-three. Then I have my presentation. Then dinner with Lane and his inner people. And you are flying away tomorrow afternoon. I leave for China on Wednesday."

"Stay here, always, have them make you 'head of New York' or something. Marry me. Stay here."

"No. Come with me to China, become my mate and never return to this city."

"No."

They broke into laughter over this last-shot solution attempt.

"So much for that."

"Nice try."

Lin paused to catch her courage.

"I am saying goodbye to you in six hours."

Georg stopped breathing. Lin sat up in her chair and put her head close to his.

"Over by the elevator. In six hours. Do not see me to the street, do not see me to the hotel, no dinner out tonight."

"Can't I put you in the cab on Central Park South?"

"No. Our last kiss must be private."

"Do you think we have the courage to part this way, with no plans, no promises?"

"Yes. And no lessening of this feeling."

Georg sat back in his chair. He looked out over Central Park as if to discover an alternate exit from harsh reality behind a tree. Eventually, failing, he looked in her eyes again.

"I can stay emotionally erect for six hours. How about you?"

They laughed with relief over this.

"Once more, I must ask something of you Georg. I risk it."

"Ask it, Lin Xin Qian."

"Print out the prelude for me, the one that came out of you after I grieved for my ancestors. Take me to the piano this afternoon. Show me how to play out the melody. I am going to find an upright piano in China and put it in my house in Wuhan, Hubei Province."

The elevator open, Lin's suitcase and office storage boxes on board, the moment of adieu arrived.

Four hands entwined, caressed, grasped together. Then Lin lifted his hands, pressing lips to them tenderly. She raised her face to his, letting fall on it the full measure of radiance shining from his beautiful eyes.

Even at so final an ending the sensation of forever flooded them, aching in its cruel truth; as so they promised once before in the night, and no less now, each desired the other entirely, naked in this world.

Arms enfolded, mouths rushed together sealing two persons, undiminished.

Monday

Mark and Lauren found just enough time for a great goodbye at Logan Airport in Boston. This included croissants and poached eggs at one particular restaurant in the terminal and glances over coffee evoking erotic recollections of the night just past, tinged with the sweet melancholy of *au revoir*.

"Should I regret not going with you again?" she whispered after a silence.

"Please don't. Or I'll drag you along."

"How else can I let you know about this tugging in my chest?"

"Put it in the next kiss."

"Okay," she said smiling, settling into satisfaction.

"You've been planning this backwoods thing for a long time, it'll be great for you."

"Yes. But if you get stuck out there more than a week, I am coming to fetch you home," she said, full of coquetry. "I'll be packin' a Malibu bikini."

They walked away from the restaurant toward his departure gate. Mark could barely keep smiles off his face. He was ready, so ready for this adventure in California. He had won the confidence of two authorities on his talent. He possessed a bomb of a secret weapon. He would be on unavoidable display once Georg's showcase exploded. And beside him walked a desirable woman who longed for him.

There was one thing, however.

"I am not sure what Georg will be like by the time I have dinner with him in Santa Monica tonight."

"A broken heart," Lauren said.

"He could be mad."

"Mark, you can't fix their situation."

"Guess not."

"They went in with eyes open," she said.

"Georg has the ability to not see obvious things even if his eyes are open. I guess it's the opposite part of his talent to see things that are very unobvious."

"I never thought of it that way. He can read what's inside, for sure."

Mark's flight began boarding. They moved to a far corner of the gate area to touch and to search each other's face for happiness. They told each other their love, right out loud. They filled up right to the brink of tears. They kissed, both tugging inside. Then Mark pulled out of her arms, turned to enter the jetway, the last to board.

Georg blinked awake at dawn.

He did not move, laying on his back, aware of the graying of the bedroom walls and faint sounds of weekday traffic building on the street far below. As he lay there it began to rain, which seemed like harsh piling-on.

This should be the moment he would touch her awake, would pull her body to him, would find her mouth, would kindle the wanting, taking, joining.

His bed was starkly empty of such possibility.

He could feel the weight of that which came into existence in the night, a new composition, the most awful ever to flow from his being. It saturated him. Jerking out of bed and before anything else, he went into the salon, sat naked at the keyboard and played it. It hurt so much he considered deleting the digital file from his computer, banishing it into the void.

But no. There was another surge in him, warning him to not avoid, not deny, not put down the pain. He walked downstairs to the guestroom in which she had slept only that first night but which had held her things. Drawers slid open, empty. Only a faint hint of her perfume lingered.

"That scent is going to haunt me," he mumbled out loud.

Just as he turned to leave, something caught his eye lying on a chair in the corner. It was the black swimsuit. He walked over to it, aware of a notecard atop it.

Please keep this, a very on-the-nose
remembrance of swimming in your pool at odd hours.

Dazed, he meandered through the kitchen, a place where the thought of eating seemed ludicrous, then up the stairs, drawn inexorably to the Bösendorfer. He opened the hinged piano bench and softly folded the swimsuit inside.

Standing there, fully aware of the price of doing so yet caught in the surge, his hand reached for the control of his auto-play system, loaded and ready for execution of the new composition.

He clicked it on.

Again the piece pulled him all the way to the bottom of grief. How easy it had been to capture it in the night; it just poured out. Grateful for the digital capture, in no condition to write anything down by hand. A grimace; the appropriate idiom did not amuse: 'he played his heart out.' Just poured out because I was the music, I was not pretending, I was this pain.

Georg let the piece continue to the end. The silence afterward impacted worse than the final sad notes drifting away into dust. He sat there for minutes in it, paying the price.

Then two things:

He heard something new. Only a glimmer, an emotional spark. He realized instantly it was the next one, the last one. Prelude No. 10.

And in answer to the pain of the awful music from the night of the empty bed, which he would never delete, which he now knew to be Prelude No. 9, he sent himself a message.

"This is not right. You should do something about it."

Georg exited the FedEx office moving fast through wet streets, umbrella deployed. The packages of scores, annotations, CDs and audio files for *Amaru Youpanki* would now fly their way to Bucchi in Boston and Amy Santos at City Opera in Los Angeles. He was driven to speed his march back to Central Park South for one reason: the new prelude was breaking out, he must be at the keyboard. Must.

Nevertheless, the case of the missing femme would not be denied.

"We did not actually break up," he said to the sidewalk.

Then he awarded himself the time right up to arriving back at the salon to specifically imagine what he could do. He visualized himself living in China. That sent him screaming inside, so alien, so distant from his power. He reviewed every argument she had presented, one by one, for him living there. Still screaming at the end of the list.

The visualization of her living in the United States? As soon as Georg took up looking at the world through the eyes of Lin Xin Qian, his blood ran cold. The U.S. would be just as alien to her as China would be to him. She speaks English fantastically well, yet the sound of it relentlessly surrounding her and the absence of her own tongue in her ear must be taxing. Alien.

Meanwhile, China contained the bed of her family, her city, thousands of years of culture of which her father was a scholar. Add to that the passionate drive to rectify the wrong done by the communists. Add the reality of the root philosophy to which she cleaves: the U.S. was becoming more collectivist, China more capitalist.

On top of all this, the position of Lin herself. She is a big person. She is a soldier on a team, plus she commands a team herself. They have a mission. She has obligations to them, to the mission, and responsibilities to do her duty. Someone committed to a cause greater than herself. A big person.

Against this, what could he say? "Stay with me, I am

handsome and I can play the piano."

Although nauseated by the seemingly obvious conclusion, belief and hope persisted in his core. He stopped evading the truth. He was more than a handsome piano player. The ideals at the heart of his compositions mattered in the world, importantly, a cause in himself and larger than. The thought at the front of his being as he furled the umbrella in the lobby of his tower fired his resolve:

'I am just as big as Lin Xin Qian.'

In the salon above Central Park, the phone rang. The returning Georg exited the elevator just in time and moved quickly to grab the call.

"Hello."

"Good morning, Georg, it's Benjamin. You are still at your apartment?"

"Yes. My plane does not leave for hours yet."

"I have to talk to you for ten minutes or so. Can you talk now?"

"Shoot."

"Something has drifted into range of my hearing, Georg, about *The Preludes*."

"What?"

"Well, I've been putting out feelers for your concerto, as you know."

"Yes. Thought about it a lot. It came to me clearly I need to get a great pianist hooked on it."

"There's someone actively working against you, I haven't found out the name yet. All I know is that a letter arrived at Chrystie Street Rep addressed to Michael Gaetano, suggesting he was ill-advised to give you his stage for *The Preludes*."

"How did you find this out?"

"Michael called me. He said he wanted to talk with me before speaking to you. Is the contract signed?"

"Yes. But why would a letter disturb him. It's just a recital of new preludes."

"Michael would not reveal the name of the writer. He said, however, it was a highly connected person known to have mojo with many reviewers. An 'influence celebrity in music circles' Michael called him."

"This sounds like Arthur Renaud."

"That's what I thought, but maybe not. The letter referenced your 1998 recital, the sonata and variations, and the reviews, and also repeated criticism of the concerto, your first concerto two years ago, in 1999. How these things spread so quickly …"

"What about them, the critics hated those pieces, so what?"

"The slant Michael conveyed to me was that he was being warned that giving you a platform would be seen as a serious embarrassment to him by the 'contemporary classical music world' because you – and I wrote this down – 'persist in codifying content and structure in disparaged, elitist and trivial modalities.'"

"Fucking bullshit."

"This person is warning Michael he himself is going to be downgraded, that all other projects and events at Chrystie Street would look cheaper if you are in the mix. Certainly it is a shot across the bow that your preludes are going to be slammed by the critics. Michael said there was a snipe line in the letter about the hubris of thinking any reputable orchestra would touch any future piano concerto. Michael said the word 'amateur' was in this letter. Twice."

"Benjamin, I am sorry you are dragged into this, it is between myself and Michael Gaetano. I will call him shortly."

"Will you call me right back?"

"Yes."

"At first I didn't want to tell you about this right before your plane …"

"You did it right. I'm hanging up now, I'll call you. Goodbye."

"Goodbye, Georg."

Georg tossed the cordless on the sofa, grabbed a lung full of air and screamed with all he could muster from the gut. After a moment of freezing, he jumped to the piano. A brilliant passage with an unabashedly romantic melody poured forth. He stood up next to the piano and let off another drastic scream.

He stepped over to the west-facing glass wall, slid open the door and stepped out onto the deck, shaking his head. The rain had paused.

Georg stood at the railing for many minutes. He had known the blowback would be arriving and now it was in his face. He would have to fight much harder this time, just as Benjamin foretold.

"So be it," he said out loud.

It required many minutes, getting calm. Steely calm. If a venue refused him in New York, he would find another. If all the venues in New York refused him, he would have to venture somewhere else to make a splash. That was something he had not been willing to do last time around. This time: not to abandon the idea of New York, but perhaps to head back to town with a hit on his hands. He stood there, New York City at his feet, and deliberately gauged the temperature of his resolve and determination. It was fierce.

In a flash, he realized that one location out of town was, in fact, China. A shudder ran through his body. It was hope, bitter irony, pain and refusal together.

He whipped all the strife of this day and his broken heart into a frenzy of single minded purpose: to strike back, strike a blow for himself as an artist. He picked up the phone and cancelled his flight to Los Angeles. Then he called his lawyer.

Three hours later, Michael Gaetano, director of Chrystie Street Repertory Theatre, sat at his working desk on the stage. In front of the desk, confronting him, stood Georg flanked by another man, Georg's lawyer.

Gaetano stared at the document in front of him, shaking his head.

"I still don't get it. Am I stupid?"

"I assure you it is exactly what it says, and what I have explained," said Georg.

"You will tear up your contract for the date to play those preludes and sign a hold-harmless discharging your right to sue me?" asked Gaetano.

"Yes. It is already signed. We have it here."

"I don't see how you can win such a suit anyway, I just changed my mind, that's all."

Georg's counsel interjected.

"As Mr. Wojciechowski's lawyer, I assure that not only could we sue, we would win and force you to give us the date. You would have to pay my fees, and I am expensive. You should entertain no illusion that we would not aggressively pursue that track, at the very least causing you as much grief and bad publicity as possible."

"And all I have to do is sign this agreement and you will go away?"

"Yes."

Gaetano waved his arms and laughed in disbelief. "But this agreement just states that I will never attempt to speak to Mr. Wojciechowski, or book him for performance, or allow any other person to perform his music on my stage, or ever profit in any way from his compositions."

"That is correct," said Georg.

"You are a complete idiot. Who do you think you are? I should wipe my ass with this."

"Sign it."

Gaetano signed with disdain. "What an asshole. I am going to spread this story all over town."

"I am counting on that."

As soon as the document was signed, the lawyer rushed to witness it. Georg rapidly tore off one copy and threw it down on the desk. He gestured to the lawyer, who handed the hold-harmless document to Gaetano.

"That is all."

They spun around and exited rapidly. Gaetano was left smirking at his desk. Then a wave of anxiety flit across his face. He picked up the agreement and read it again, worried.

Outside, Georg's lawyer raised his hand to hail a cab.

"Sorry you had to go through that," said Georg. "Thanks for acting so fast, right in the middle of a Monday."

"Not a problem. I deal with weaklings all the time. I didn't even wince. I don't get to see such gestures often. Ever, actually. Lydia was right about you, Georg."

He shook Georg's hand, then jumped into the cab that

had answered his hail. Georg raised his hand as well and snared another of the yellow chariots.

Headed uptown on Sixth Avenue his preludes would not let him alone. The painful one played over and over in a loop yet could not inundate the emergence of this new thing, this last one. At the pit of the stomach lay the realization that just as his opus neared completion, his venue to announce them to the world had been blasted away.

As had the love of his life.

With great sardonic amusement he arrived at a prototypical point for an artist beset with just such monumental woe piled up all in one day: 'I need a drink.' Immediately on admitting this, the irony doubled; he knew just the place.

"Changed my mind," he announced to the cabbie. "Harry Cipriani's Bar in the Sherry-Netherland Hotel."

As befits a swank saloon, 'Harry' provided a phone at the table. With one eye watching out onto the corner of Fifth and Fifty-Ninth, Georg fetched Amy Santos in Los Angeles. It was nearing five o'clock, but only a little past lunchtime on the West Coast.

Earlier, prior to his adventure at Chrystie Street Rep, Mark and then Angela had taken his calls from the salon, Mark being equipped with his big mobile and having safely disembarked under the palm trees at LAX. Georg informed them both that he was not in transit westward, needed a few more days in New York. They were both disappointed but quickly climbed on board the shift of the plan to Friday. Mark was especially understanding when he heard about the traitorous Gaetano pulling the rug out from beneath his friend.

"Is the loss of the venue the only reason you are changing the date of our meeting out here?" Mark asked forthrightly.

"No, not the only."

"Is she gone?"

"Not back to China, but gone, yes."

"What are you going to do?"

"Something."

"Georg, do not abandon the preludes."

"I cannot. They are screaming in my ear."

"Thank goodness," said Mark, and they hung up.

Sitting now at Harry's Bar, Amy Santos came on the line, still at her desk at City Opera of Los Angeles.

"You've heard by now I want to move our showcase planning meeting to Friday?"

"Yes, Angela told me. That is actually better for me."

"That's good, Amy. I tend to push and I pushed for tomorrow. That was too rushed."

"I am really excited and Friday is perfect. Is Mark bringing materials?"

"Yes, and this morning I sent some from here as well. They'll be on your desk tomorrow."

"This is good."

"Amy, have you been to China?"

"Yes. Mr. Corbin took me twice as assistant before he retired from singing. As a matter of fact, I am going ahead soon."

"You are?"

"He wants to produce *Turandot* in Beijing and other cities in 2002 or 2003. A different sort of production than the big one in 1998 that Zubin Mehta conducted. I am to scout locations and stir up interest."

"Wow."

"Chinese cast and orchestra, and not with himself in the role of Calàf, which he sang so many times. He'd love to have this one last tour before retiring from all music for good, but just to oversee it, not perform."

"Can I have a little more of your time? I need to ask you about opera and classical music in China."

"Okay."

Ten minutes later Georg finished his call and drained the last drop of his scotch. Clearly it was too early for the arrival of Miss Happy Money; she would be hours yet with her giant agenda this day. He considered ordering another Dalwhinnie. Although this bar invoked its namesake in Paris, where Hemmingway and other artists prodigiously put away their liquor while nursing wounds from women, the irony was no longer working. He was too angry.

Obtaining a blank memo pad with the bar's logo at the top, he scribbled out a note, jotting it with attitude. He paid his tab, strolled twenty feet into the lobby of the Sherry-Netherland and arranged for the note to be sealed and slid under the door of the guest from China, who was expected to be out a few more hours this evening and scheduled to abide just two more nights at this splendid address.

Lin arrived at the Sherry after eight o'clock. Her stoic face while marching through the lobby belied secreted victories. Her presentation had shaken up some of Lane's people. She mentally added 'in a good way' when she recalled the looks on their faces.

♦ Lin's Presentation, page 145 ♦

Another tagline accompanied her up to her room: 'I've finally got that billion in my back pocket.'

The note on the floor of her room:

No one next to me in bed. Dresser empty of girl pajamas.
Gray skies, dreary rain. New prelude in the middle of the
night, sad as hell. You left your swimsuit behind.
I did not go to Los Angeles.

At nine in the evening Georg came to the end of waiting. 'That's enough,' his motion out of his chair seemed to say. He donned street clothes and a crisp-weather jacket, grabbed an umbrella and departed the apartment.

Below, his march east on Central Park South bore the markings of an assault on fate, at night in this magnificent city where such undertakings are not considered foolish, streets wet and streaked with long quavering reflections of traffic lights, braced against an early September chill, to challenge for the championship. He surely championed the correct cause, flying its flag at the fore, he believed. The tower of the Sherry-Netherland Hotel rose directly ahead, the only landmark required.

He crossed Fifth Avenue. He approached the door of the hotel. From the portal emerged the familiar form with long black hair flying free, animated by swift movement full of purpose.

They jerked to a stop in front of one another.

"No," she said.

"Where are you going?"

"No, we said no more. And you are in Los Angeles for *Amaru*."

"I changed my mind."

"Yes I found your stupid note. You went against your promise, put the toothpaste back in the tube, betrayed your friends' gifts and gave up on your mission. To chase a girl."

"Yes."

"For a girl. Ridiculous wrong person."

"She is worth it."

"No girl wants a man who gives up."

"You are a woman."

"Please move out of the way."

"Where are you going?"

"To China. To carry on my mission."

"There is a new prelude now. Since last night."

"Fine, I will tell you where I am going, walking in the rain to Lydia's tower, to give Georg Wojciechowski my anger."

"I am headed there myself. I'll give you a lift."

She did not reduce the antagonism in her face. His held only quiet determination. As if on cue it resumed raining. Rather than open his umbrella he thrust his arm in the air which instantly caused a cab to swerve to them and pull to a stop. Georg ushered Lin into the back seat, feeling her arm stiff and resisting. The cabbie waited for other traffic to clear, slanted across lanes of Fifth Avenue and made the turn west. Rain poured down in torrents, crashing on the roof of the taxi.

Lin lay on the floor beneath the piano. Georg's Prelude No. 9 lay upon her soul.

"Again," she said.

This time instead of playing it he stood up from the bench, triggered the playback and came around to join her beneath, taking her body in his arms. They held each other in silence until it nearly played out.

♦ Prelude No. 9 ♦

"It hurts."

"Yes," he agreed. The piece concluded, winding down to its dim sad end.

"Then why do we keep listening to it? Play it again."

"Not yet. It hurts, and it is the truth. We want the truth, that's why we listen."

"China is my home."

"You've said that many times now. Even though it's true, I'm not going to make it easy for you. I want you to stay here and live with me."

He worked his way out of her arms, out from beneath the piano and reached down to pull her upright. He walked over to the piano bench and lifted it open, pulling out a garment that he gently put in her hands: the black swimsuit.

"I did postpone my showcase meeting in Los Angeles to chase a girl. But I did not abandon my mission."

"I know."

Georg related the events of the day, the backstab at Chrystie Street and his magnificent off-balance response, plus his reschedule of the *Amaru Youpanki* meeting to Friday in Los Angeles.

"The most important thing is the new prelude. The one after this sad one. It is exploding out. After I wrote you that note sitting in Harry's Bar I walked back here. It took possession of me all evening, until I couldn't take it anymore and had to go find you."

"Play it."

"No. Not yet. The story inside it is not finished."

"Then how can you be writing it already?"

"It knows itself better than I know it. This music has a life of its own. It's Prelude Number 10, the final composition of the opus."

"It will not change anything."

"Lin, I want nothing more than to sit here and listen to the story of all you accomplished today, on an international level, even if it slaps me in the face how big you are and how much it might appear I'm in over my head. It's billions against forty-thousand and a few tunes. I don't care."

"It will not change anything."

"At least you will see that I understand you. I know about your responsibilities, your mission, your power in it."

She dropped the swimsuit to the floor.

"You have no idea about responsibility to others, about family loyalty, about saving a country from monsters."

That was pain more than anger. He must smash it.

"What did you think this is, *Roman Holiday*? You have to take off your pajamas and put on my pajamas for that to be true."

"What?"

"Spend a day in my pants. Then try saying those things to me."

"You are crazy."

"We are screening that film tomorrow. That hurt, what you said."

She walked toward the elevator vestibule. "I will not be here tomorrow."

He followed her, grabbed the swimsuit off the floor, stopped her.

"Hear me out. Two more things."

"It will not change anything."

"I promise you I respect and honor who is Lin Xin Qian of China, your choices. Never change this. But you don't have to turn down the other, the personal pleasure in your soul. The fire for yourself. It's not 'either/or.' It's 'both/and.' You have to fight hard to get both."

She did not answer back, but he saw her eyes lose the hard edge around the corners.

"Second, we have to honor the choice we made. To fall in love."

"You think we chose it?"

"Yes. The world says that we don't chose whom we

love, but we do. We do. I was thunderstruck by you from the start. You know that. For god's sake you wanted to rip the clothes off of me in Lincoln Center."

"Sex."

"No. Not just sex. It was everything already, right then. But Lin, I am going to say this, it's the most important thing: later we gave our consent. We knew the stakes on so many levels. The danger. But we let go, we chose to fall all the way in love. We are not fools. We are smart. You have to believe we were wise, deeply wise, deeper than words or anything, and we made it happen. We can't go against that wisdom. We have to be together."

Lin honored with her courage to not turn her face away; she accepted all he said without flinching. It went all the way in. Georg watched new hope and new pain grow in her visage, making him love her all the more. Tears rolled from her eyes now.

"It is time for your family to go international. You are a leader, not a functionary. Lead from New York City."

Lin removed her eyes from his. She turned away and walked to the elevator. He stayed right behind her.

"Wait, you forgot this," he said, holding out the swim-suit to her.

She shook her head slowly. "Keep it," she whispered.

She pressed the button that opened the waiting eleva-tor. He moved in front of her. She brushed past him. Georg jumped in as well, his finger on a button keeping the door open.

"We'll throw it away and swim naked all the time, then," he said.

"You are breaking my heart. I love you so much I will break, to possess you, to stay with you, to make you happy. To leave my home. But you would not love the broken Xin very long. The unhappy Xin."

He very slowly exited the elevator. He did not take his eyes off hers for one second. He released the door, left her in there, in the company of her ancestors, her family and all of China.

As the elevator door closed, he shot out one more

zinger.

"Too late. There is no happy Xin without me in her bed."

The elevator began its descent. Instantly Georg intercomed down to the lobby. Allan's relief person, Stan, was on duty.

"Yes, Mr. Wojciechowski?"

"Stan, this is an emergency. You have to do something for me. Do you have a pen and paper?"

"Sure, wait … okay. Is everything okay?"

"Yes but we have to act fast. Miss Lin is on the way down. You have to write a note from me and hand it to her, okay?"

"Oh. Okay."

"Do not be afraid if she acts upset. Just get out of the way. Quickly."

"Okay … wow."

"Now write this down …"

Stanley clicked off the intercom. At least this is not a boring night, he thought, reading the note he had just hastily written.

The elevator opened. The striking Asian woman burst out, walking fast, looking dangerous. He came around the front of his desk.

"Miss Lin?"

"What?"

"Mr. W. wanted me to give you this note."

She yanked it from his hand.

> *Come back up here or I will fly to China tomorrow and*
> *ask your father's permission to court you.*
> *And how much is the dowry. Not bluffing.*

"*Sei ham ga chan, sei puk gai!*" she screamed.

Stan's eyes went huge. He scurried back behind his desk in terror. Miss Lin stamped toward the door of the building. Suddenly she froze in place. With a frightening scream and black hair flying she spun and charged back to the elevator like the murderous Queen of the Night. As she passed Stan she snapped out her response in staccato Cantonese.

"You tell him I said '*Lnei go jeu jeu mm kup duk oh go gau.*'"

Before he could muster the courage to ask for a translation she shot into the elevator and was gone.

To get the translation of Lin's outburst
go to the Cantonese swearing page at thepreludes.com

Georg swam gracefully. He was at peace. All dice cast, all chance taken. Steam rose dramatically from the heated water's surface. It rained into the pool without letup; it seemed he swam between the drops. He noticed his strokes paced themselves to the rhythm and cadence of his new prelude, no. 10, which already seemed old to him. Old but not complete. In it flowed the heartbreak of losing her, if lost, yet more so victory in having made his voice say the truth. This is how he must live, forever.

Making a turn at the south end, a few strokes north, his eye caught sight of she whom so ardently it wished to see, moving purposefully while discarding clothing, hair flying free but taking up the rain, reaching the opposite end of the pool, entering in a shallow dive.

They swam to each other. They swam into each other's arms.

"You got him to sign that he would never make any money from you?"

"That's right. I wanted to punch his face, but this was more satisfying."

"That was magnificent. I wish I had been there."

"Then I went drinking."

"I must warn you, Mister W., I could take you up on your promise to make me happy in bed forever."

"Done."

"I called the Bösendorfer offices in Vienna today."

"What?"

Lin laughed with joy, delighted to have shocked him. "Yes, in between meetings. Additionally, we need visionaries in China. China has not had a Beethoven yet."

Which way this was going was as usual disorientingly unknown, certainly off-balance. Who the hell was winning now? All he knew so far: she was naked and in his arms.

"No, no Beethoven yet."

"You speak about finding a Mozart or Rubenstein here in New York? Never stop that. But also, perhaps his name is Tian Lio Sha, living along the Yangtze River. You might need to be his Benjamin."

Georg eyed her intently, but said nothing. Lin delivered her next surprise in typical bombshell fashion.

"I placed an order for the Bösendorfer Imperial Concert Grand Model 290, black lacquer finish, with full recording controls installed."

"No!"

Lin stood up tall in the pool with arms reaching to the pouring-out night sky and raised her high-Mandarin priestess voice over Manhattan. "Delivered to Shanghai for one hundred and seventy-three thousand fucking dollars, U.S."

"Oh my god."

"It is not for you. It is for Wuhan Philharmonic Orchestra."

"You bought it?"

"Yes."

"Can I try out my preludes on it?"

"But of course. I did not tell you about this piano earlier because I wanted to win our argument and bring you to China without using it as a bribe."

"You really bought one?"

"The billion-plus was burning a hole in my pocket. That is a correct idiom, I believe."

"Yes."

He kissed her very beautifully, very deeply.

She pulled away to look in his eyes. "Last night in my bed at the Sherry was miserable, cold and empty like a grave. I would have been disappointed if you had departed for Los Angeles without fighting for us again."

Her near-black eyes wanted to fill with tears, he believed, looking deeply into them, yet her warrior spirit forestalled any weeping: she must deliver final truths in the pouring rain.

"I could not defeat the feeling, lying there alone in that bed: if you did put up a fight, you would win me. I want you Georg."

His heart took flight. "If I had not fought again, would you have chased me down to start it?"

"Yes, but you do not know how angry a she-dragon you would have faced. I would have shown up in Los Angeles to burn your toes."

"We will stay in whichever nation does not kick the basket. Or live in both, in the world," he said.

"Yes. In both I believe. But to start, I have decided, riding up here in the elevator with your ridiculous note in my hand, when I arrive in Wuhan I am going to inform my uncle that I wish to continue as Ambassador to the United States, and he is to send me to live in New York City. I will lead from here."

Georg could not speak. His relief and joy combined into a sumptuous living dream too rich for words. It surrounded him with no less splendor than when a new melody touched him in the night, waking him from sleep and he knew he was alive.

"Where I will be happy and useful, in bed and out."

With that, Lin escaped his arms. She swam fast to the south end of the pool. Georg chased her, caught her. They embraced, standing in the end of the pool with New York City all around.

"You are crazy if you think I will ever be without you."

"Possess me everywhere in the world, and I you."

From high above Georg could be seen to release the embrace, climb out of the pool and reach an arm back to pull her out. Rain showered down on them heavier than ever.

Hand in hand, naked, they disappeared quickly into the bedroom of their penthouse in the sky.

Epilogue

The next morning, Tuesday morning, in the dawn after their plans and promises were born, rain clouds vanished and a high brilliant sky opened over Manhattan, under which Lin and Georg slept the profound sleep of victors.

They were awakened by the roar of a Boeing 767 aircraft traveling 575 miles per hour at a frighteningly low altitude, only 700 yards to the west of their bedroom. It was American Airlines Flight 11 following the Hudson River south, 5 miles and 30 seconds away from its end. The time was 8:43 a.m., Tuesday, September 11, 2001.

From their terrace they observed planes exploding in the Towers and an hour later both buildings fail, collapsing into dust.

When they discovered that it was specifically Flight 11 that had crashed into the North Tower, Lin and Georg's level of both peril and relief escalated: Mark Warren Williamson had left Lauren at the gate and boarded American Airlines Flight 11 out of Boston, but on Monday the 10th, the day before; he was safe in Los Angeles.

With no planes flying anywhere, Lin turned to monitoring the secure finalization of the one point three billion dollar funds transfer closed the prior day, now somewhat destabilized by the chaos in Manhattan. Over the next weeks Lin also joined Henry Lane in a cooperative effort to aid firms having lost people, records and offices to stay alive and begin to rebuild.

Even as conditions settled and her funds flowed properly, she communicated to her uncle by phone and letter her wish to become permanent ambassador and cultural attaché for her family to the United States, based in New York City. This was accepted provisionally, contingent on discussion when she returned to China.

Lin and Georg comforted each other, loving deeply in their aerie high above the city. All senses, all urgencies, all realities sharpened to the quick, they took full measure of healing in each other's arms. Caring for one another through pain and anger over events cemented their union.

Late in September Lin traveled to China for three weeks to affirm, plan and execute her move to new permanent offices in New York, bond with family and make promises of frequent returns to them.

At the same time Georg mounted his showcase for the opera *Amaru Youpanki* in Los Angeles. He also easily engaged a new venue in New York at which to premiere his opus, the *Ten Preludes for Piano*. He was launched.

In October 2001 they reunited on Central Park South. While the mood of their loving continued to be bruised by grief over the attack and damage to their city, still they celebrated jubilantly and affirmed their life together.

In January of 2002 Lin returned again to China. She greeted family with exuberant happiness. After embracing her, each member of the clan received introduction one by one to her life mate, the American Georg Wojciechowski, who stood at her side.

On the afternoon of their first day in Wuhan, Georg walked across the stage of a theater to where a huge and imposing piano, black lacquer with brass shining inside, a magnificent new Bösendorfer Imperial Grand, awaited an artist. He composed at the keyboard that day and later performed a concert on it, including his *Piano Concerto No. 1* which had been rejected in New York previously, accompanied by the Wuhan Philharmonic Orchestra.

During their stay in Wuhan, after some days to become acquainted, Georg asked Lin's father and mother for consent to marry their daughter. It was a formality of respect and honored as such, symbolic but significant.

During the stupendous growth of the next twelve

years, Lin and her uncle waged a campaign to leverage capital and minimize the damage of government interference throughout central China. Their efforts, and those of like-minded businessmen, maintained what freedom and productivity could be found in their civilization. Lin's role in New York made a significant contribution to this success. In many ways, for many reasons, she became a New Yorker, yet sustaining a circumstance well-known and honored: a New Yorker with dual citizenship and residency in the wide world.

In the United States, the shock of the terrorist attack in September 2001, combined with the destruction caused by Federal Reserve actions to burst the "dot-com bubble" ended a period of economic optimism. Worse, a "real estate bubble" followed, during which no agency took action, resulting in a drastic crisis and near meltdown of the world economic system in 2008.

Despite the trend of the U.S. rapidly appearing to "kick the basket" and China appearing to explode on the world with economic power, Lin and Georg retained New York as their base during the first decade of the new millennium. This was bolstered when Lydia, thrilled to have witnessed Georg's emergence and success and delighted with his chosen mate, conveyed to them the deed on the duplex apartment atop her tower on Central Park South. She passed the deed to the couple during the party celebrating their wedding.

Many journeys to China ensued. Lin was correct that classical music would burgeon in her homeland. Georg was correct that the time had arrived for her family to become international, with New York as the flagship overseas office. Both additionally discovered necessity and opportunity to journey to other nations, other cities, for other adventures.

Each time they settled into the destination bedroom of a transition, no matter where in the world, a treasured yet wary ritual unfolded.

"We're home," Georg always began.

"Yes, but we must always leave our luggage at the ready," Lin would warn.

"Travel is wonderful, but how can we shake off the dust of the road?"

"Take a shower with me," said Lin, holding her hand out to him.

2014

From above the ocean shore at night, a house alone on a low hill surrounded by sand dunes and beach grass glowed from within through many windows. Inside could be seen a huge grand piano, black lacquer with brass gleaming. Georg stood at the instrument. He switched it on and his Prelude No. 10 began to execute.

♦ Prelude No. 10 ♦

Georg walked out to join Lin on a terrace of the house. They were finely dressed as if to attend an event. Suddenly from the interior two children ran to them, a boy of nine and a girl of seven. They were also dressed for celebration, the girl attired in beautiful blue silk. All happily interacted until the children ran off back into the house.

Lin and Georg stood at the railing of the terrace. A sea breeze blew their hair. Lin leaned back against Georg. They looked out over the world together, unafraid and alive. The prelude neared its end. In its final measures every nuance of their faces spoke of peace and certainty. Lin turned to face him and threw her arms around his neck.

"This prelude thrills me every time, even these many years," she said.

"Where do you feel it?"

Lin moved against him inside the embrace. Then she lifted her lips to his ear to whisper, just as the last low note of the prelude resounded like a clap of thunder.

"Everywhere your hands love to touch me."

Extras

The Music:
Preludes 1,7,8,9,10
Carl Czerny, *School of Velocity*
Frédéric Chopin, *Etude in C Minor* op. 25 no. 12
'O soave fanciulla,' from *La Bohème* by Giacomo Puccini
Amaru's Aria
Love duet, Amaru and Quilla

The music files will be found on the website for
The Preludes
http://thepreludes.com

Scenes:

Mark/Georg Conversation at Lincoln Center

Fifteen minutes after their extraordinary interaction with Lin Xin Qian, Georg and Mark emerged from the Performing Arts Library. Georg now carried a bound folder.

"Mark?"

"What?"

"I'm going to ask you for another working session on my aria before you go to Boston."

"I thought you were working strictly on the preludes for piano?" Mark responded with bemused annoyance. "Did you give up on them?"

"No, but I can work on both. I am the prelude guy *and* the aria guy."

"What a life."

"But there's only so much opera composition I can do without tenor on board," Georg continued. "I've got to tangle with you."

"I'm marching off to my stupendous destiny," countered Mark, milking the moment, "and you want me to make quality time materialize just to feed your hobby? Hell, Boston is a week from tomorrow. Next Friday! I suppose you'll want plenty of B naturals, right? Jeez, this is a great friendship!"

They rounded the corner of the Metropolitan Opera

House, returning to the main plaza. They stopped walking.

"Friends give friends their B naturals," stated Georg flatly.

This elicited an amused disgusted sound and a dry response from his friend. "I have nothing to say to that. Nothing."

"And I'm ignoring that 'hobby' comment," threw in Georg.

"Well prove me wrong then," came the answer.

Fishing in his valise, Mark pulled out his Day-Timer. "Okay, stop right here. If this is happening I'm pinning you down right here, right now."

"Don't you have that PDA the girlfriend gave you?" quipped Georg, smiling.

"Lover. We prefer 'lover.' And you know her name."

"Okay, lover. Lauren."

"Can't stand that thing," Mark announced. "I need written." With a dubious glance at his friend, Mark consulted his book, murmuring, flipping pages. "Okay … this coming Tuesday afternoon, the fourth. That's the only way. Friday for final packing and then from LaGuardia to Logan. I'm going to have to collapse a few things back. Wait, wait … no it's okay. Tuesday. After that I have to rest my voice and then bring it up on Thursday and Friday; I'm going to need everything on Saturday in front of Carlisle and Bucchi."

"Let's make it a celebration dinner too," threw in Georg. "Will you go for that Tuesday evening? We want to send you off in grand fashion. A little party?"

Mark held Georg's eyes for a long beat. The wind on the plaza stirred his short hair. In a few seconds it became a significant stare-down.

"What?" asked Georg.

"I want the world premiere."

Georg nodded. "I see."

"Let's put it on the table," Mark continued. "Brutal honesty. You are hoping to have a famous tenor for the premiere of this aria, make a sensation."

"Yes."

"And I'm not famous. But now I want it straight. Leaving aside fame, can anyone in the world nail it better than I can?"

Georg came up erect to face this challenge.

"No," he answered.

"I want the world premiere."

Georg gave his answer with irony. "It might be at a recital in which the brilliant young tenor wows the world and makes an aria famous."

"And at which a great aria makes the career of a tenor," finished Mark, then pulled back a little and set himself to deliver a serious follow-on. "Okay then. Unless you forbid it, or talk me out of it for good reason, I'm going to throw this aria in my auditions in Boston and Los Angeles. You might not think this is ever going to be part of a real opera, but I know this is a real aria, right now."

Georg looked off to the side, considering briefly, then nodded assent. They shook on it, although Georg was not completely happy.

"You'll work up the backing track for me, on a disk?"

"I'll have it for you Tuesday."

"Do you think it's ever going to be an opera? How far along are you? When can I see the libretto? I'm nuts just having this one aria."

Georg flashed him a savage look.

"Magnificent though it may be," Mark amended.

"When we go to work Tuesday I'll fill you in."

"Well, I just wish you were in play too, like I am."

"When we go to work Tuesday I'll fill you in," repeated Georg, irritated and dismissive.

"Okay," said Mark, smiling and letting go. "Okay, then, to the party, too."

"You got it. I'll set it up.

They resumed walking. Georg changed the subject.

"Why are you going to Sante Fe? The season is already over."

"Yes, but I've been invited to attend a workshop, gratis, run by the artistic director of the Sante Fe Opera. They are looking for new blood, new singers, new ideas. Anyway, he's sticking around. They are having meetings about next summer's choices, anyway, and how to keep the damn thing afloat financially. Not enough Puccini. Puccini fills the seats every time."

"Speaking of whom," injected Georg, "he is the reason I needed to pick up this score at the library: research."

"On Puccini?"

"Yes. *Girl of the Golden West*, you know, where she saves him from hanging at the end and they ride off into the sunset. I'm trying to solve the 'Puccini dead end,' how to write a dramatic love story with a happy ending. *'Girl'* is his best try. Puccini died before finishing *Turandot* and he was having plenty of trouble with that ending."

They were now walking parallel to the Metropolitan Opera House approaching posters under glass of the six productions currently playing in rotation. They stopped at the first poster.

"Ah, here we go, the cavalcade of the human condition per the Metropolitan Opera. Season starts in late September, only a couple of weeks to go," said Georg.

Resuming a favorite game of theirs, 'Flame the Opera,' Georg started: "*Eugene Onegin*, I'll take this one: 'Flirting, scheming, jealousy, manipulation, affairs, bad marriage, wrong decisions among the purposeless upper class. There's a duel, broken hearts and suicide at the end.'"

Now it was Mark's turn: "*Wozzeck*. I tried to study it once. The recitative is gruesome. No arias, really. But this is a classic of the repertoire now, the Met has given it over fifty times. 'Everything is alienation, failure, pain, ending in insanity and murder. This is the fault of the capitalists, the underclass is the victim.'"

They looked at each other with flat resignation that such an opera has a following, then laughed at the absurdity.

Moving to the poster for *Idomene*, Mark showed an affectionate smile. "Ah, Mozart pulls out the *deus ex machina*. It should have been a tragedy of karma from the Trojan War, refusal to obey the gods and jealous manipulations of various women. Instead, Idomeneo ends up with the right girl by a miracle of forgiveness at the end, because love triumphs."

Georg's turn brought him to a good place: "*La Bohème*, always *La Bohème*, over eleven hundred performances by the Met. The genius of Act I, completely. In the middle of the ordinary, the fantastic can actually occur. *Verismo*."

"Well," Mark interjected, "I can tell you from the tenor's point of view, the high C in 'Che gelida manina' is devastating. If you hit it, how can she say no; she'll get in your bed immediately. If there is even the slightest doubt, you throw another C later on, on the last note of the duet, instead of the written A."

"You certainly have that C, Mark."

"Yes, Lauren believes in it."

They laughed together over this seduction verity, one to which Puccini himself would surely subscribe. Then, as they walked away from the poster of *La Bohème*, Mark couldn't contain himself. His voice rang out at full power with the first lines of the famous duet.

"O soave fanciulla, o dolce viso
di mite circonfuso alba lunar
in te, vivo ravviso il sogno
ch'io vorrei sempre sognar!"

Mark broke off his little solo. Scattered applause arose from around the plaza, to which Mark made a bow. As they moved to the next poster, Mark threw in a final comment: "Most popular, most beloved opera, but it is really only about one thing: death."

Georg pulled Mark to a stop.

"I'm glad we settled it. Make it your aria. I'm satisfied. Make Bucchi's hair stand up on the back of his neck, will you?"

"I think you should consider an alternative reality. The premiere of your great aria might not be in a recital."

"No?"

"Instead, at an actual performance of the actual opera. I will be in the lead, on stage, with a packed house buzzing with buzz. Things can move faster than you think, Georg. Instead of a few arias floating along, this could be an opera, on the stage, with the audience going nuts. People love the operas on these posters, but they're starving for new ones this great. Without the big bummer at the end."

Georg looked off into the distance. He remained silent, visualizing the imagined day. As always, anxiety blossomed alongside the thrill; the dragons that must be slain to make his opera real loomed nearby, ferocious and hot.

After a few seconds, Mark returned to his impaling of the Met's offerings.

"*Norma*: A horrible love triangle mixed in with superstitious religion and political oppression. The result is double self-immolation, literally.

"*Luisa Miller*: True love ruined by an envious powerful woman, ending in double suicide by poison in the third act."

Throwing up his hands, Mark finished on a note of ridiculous exasperation. "So, except for Mozart's miracle, all love ends in untimely death. See what I mean?"

They turned to take in the entire front of the Met, especially the six posters standing in a row.

"Opera is deadly for lovers," Georg said sadly.

Mark looked at his friend with challenge. "Yes. You should do something about it."

The Battle in Bed

"How many pianos in China?" Lin demanded at the first sign of his eyelids fluttering open.

"I don't know. A hundred thousand. What time is it?"

"Seventy-six point six million."

"What?"

"How many times is a Beethoven, Mozart or Brahms symphony given in China every year? Or a major concerto by your romantic heroes?"

"Lin ..."

"How many times?"

"Well, visiting orchestras ..."

"Chinese orchestras. And soloists."

"Five?"

"One hundred and seventy-eight."

"What's going on?"

"I received an email from one of my staff people in China, someone I sent out on a research project."

"No, I mean what's going on?"

"I am catching you off-balance."

"Really. Your favorite thing. Even at dawn on a Sunday in bed naked with your friend."

"Yes. I am not going to make this easy for you. I am going to make you love my home in China."

There was a pause. She pulled the comforter tighter around her shoulders.

"What is going to happen in Washington now?" she

resumed.

"You are zigzagging."

"Stay with me. You have a gigantic continent with few people and small population growth. If it were not for immigration, you would have only a slow, very slow growth. You can not imagine how weak that appears to China. Do you not love your country enough to have babies and fill it up?"

"That's a wild thing to say."

"I stand by it. My province, Hubei Province?"

"Yes?"

"It is the same size as your Missouri. It is also in the middle of the nation, with the country's most important river going through it. It has an important city, Wuhan, like your St. Louis. What is the population of Missouri?"

"Eleven million?"

"Five point five million. Hubei Province, sixty million people.

"You built a completely new industry, desktop computers and high-tech. This exploded productivity on the world. Now your Fed chairman has decided to not let those tech startups destined for failure die naturally, but rather to deliberately destroy the entire risk-taking culture in tech, has jacked up the cost of money six times since the summer of 1999 and just in this past two years sent it into hell. The problem is, the rest of the economy is taking damage along with his assassination of high-tech. You have kicked off this new millennium with an act of self-destruction.

"You have lost heavy industry. Detroit is nearly comatose. Your young people hate entry-level jobs or craft-skill jobs and want to be paid seventy thousand right after college for their brains. But college is glorified high school with beer and sex all day long.

"What critical skills do they have? You abandoned the proper way to teach reading, you have a shameful literacy rate, your math and science learning is spiraling down, you teach them 'there are no absolutes' and they believe it, and translate to 'I do not really need to know anything.' Even retail and service are low grade here. Agriculture is vulnerable because of addiction to subsidy and debt-driven finance. Your energy development is in the toilet."

"Nice."

"You demonized and abandoned nuclear power and no one can build an oil refinery, or dam a river for hydro. Your entrepreneurs are hobbled by a dump truck full of regulation and prohibition. I could go on and on. You are losing ground fast. You are paralyzed. Why? Because you betrayed your core philosophy.

"The United States was meant to be a nation of gold, enterprise, achievement, upward mobility, prosperity and wide open freedom and property rights. Instead you have grafted on cartelism and socialism. In the world's greatest capitalist nation, ninety percent of your intellectuals hate capitalism."

"Yes."

"And those same intellectuals do not talk about or champion freedom."

"No."

"Gold is not supposed to tarnish, but you managed it."

"You are suggesting that I keep only one foot in the basket," he said.

"Yes. I have not even spoken about your chosen field, in which it is suicide to write a beautiful melody for crying out loud."

He smiled inside over her idioms. He was desperate for coffee.

"Yes, I do love New York City," she continued. "I love the United States. That is why I am so angry about this, all the more so because you still have the one thing the rest of the world lacks."

"What?"

"There is optimism. Not fatalism, like the rest of the world, optimism. Your people, not the intellectuals, remain connected to the idea of freedom, the love of freedom as nowhere else in the world. You have never been beaten down, utterly defeated and demoralized. More than any other people, Americans are free of envy and hate for people who achieve and become wealthy."

"You are making my argument for me with that," he said. "Don't you want to live where this feeling keeps going?"

"Optimism is not enough."

"So what about China?" he said.

"You know what I think. We have the only substantial free-market capitalism in the world. Maybe India, to a lesser degree. We used to have a nation of a billion: eight-hundred million peasants and two hundred million in towns and cities. Now we have nearly a billion slowly prospering farmers and three hundred million entrepreneurs, knowledge workers, professionals and capitalist go-getters, like you had during your Golden Age of Capitalism. The government is staying hands off."

Okay, that's enough. This woman is a fine battler. But now it was his turn.

"But Lin, every socialist all the way back to Marx knows, and has written, that first there must be a bourgeoisie, Petite Bourgeoisie and Grand Bourgeoisie, to create the wealth, before it can be seized and distributed. Your seizing and clamping down could happen any time. China's official orthodox government-controlled banking and building and economic growth? Corrupt and dirty. It's not free market capitalism. You have to stop calling what is happening in China 'free market capitalism.' And you have to face that no matter what the issues here, the United States is still the most powerful and productive capitalist nation."

She pouted, something he had never seen before. It was astonishing.

"And don't get me started about the fatalism, superstition, class envy and fear of individualism, of sticking out, that you have told me about," he added.

"So I must also keep only one foot in the basket," she admitted.

"Yes."

There was a long pause, thinking about the world. Lin touched his back and shoulders lovingly.

"Georg, I know you love your country. You love it dearly."

"Yes."

"But it may be dying."

"I know that. It could collapse like the Soviet Union someday."

"Mine could commit suicide at any moment," she confessed.

They looked deeply in each other's eyes to discover who had won.

"But China is my home," she said.

"The U.S. is mine. New York is still the greatest city in the world."

They were too exhausted to argue any more, or to make love. Instead they folded together and fell back to sleep.

Lin's Presentation

Monday afternoon when Lin entered a medium-size conference room, fifteen high-functioning people greeted her, including Henry Lane. Lin was dressed seriously but elegantly, looking like a million bucks, but a muted million, in an exquisitely tailored, understated business suit, hair perfect in a simple, tight chignon. She wore little makeup.

Lin was to use her white board, nothing digital, so ample light streamed in from north-facing fenestration. Lane got people's attention from the podium and everyone sat in place.

"Welcome everyone," he began. "My special appreciation for those who flew in from the Midwest and the Coast. We have a challenging guest this afternoon. I know it is already a long day but if anyone is dragging, you probably won't be, very soon. I had to schedule our speaker at this time because of closing a major transaction with her this morning.

"I know you are sensing there will be something unusual happening here today. This is not a typical marketing session nor a division shakeup or anything operational. It is philosophic. I want you to know, additionally, that I consider the subject of critical importance to the company, and to you personally. I mean critical. The combined firepower in this room has hardly been concentrated like this, ever. Do the math on the value of your combined time. These two hours are costing tens of thousands. I intend for them to bring us millions.

"Our guest is Miss Lin Xin Qian from the nation of China. She does not represent the current government of China. She is here with a team to negotiate with us an important finance project for infrastructure development across the center and west of her nation. That is ongoing, the first funding occurring this morning. However, during our discussions, I unearthed something more valuable than gold in Lin. She knows something we need to know. Just to put it in perspective, a casual comment at dinner two weeks ago turned into a five hour shakedown. I repeat, Lin held me spellbound for five hours. And stood up to my A-game grilling."

A few murmurs and expletives greeted this information. Lane let that be Lin's introduction. He sat down. Lin rose to the podium to begin.

The first hour of Lin's presentation had passed.

Her thesis: pockets of profit gone untapped because of the persistence and dominance of appealing to a low common denominator in both price and quality. The usual culprits as tools for the appeal: fear and sex. She provided many examples, both in companies founded or funded by their bank and many others in the general marketplace.

"If you appeal to fear and sex, you garner a certain reflexive response. Purchases motivated by these emotions depend on the consumer overlooking lack of quality and lack of rational need. They say 'oh well, gotta have it.' "

A few laughs circled the room due both to recognition of the syndrome and the disorientation of an Americanism like this coming from the mouth of so exotic a speaker.

Lin made it clear she did not suggest full abandonment of these all-too-successful angles, but rather to overlay with another approach, a quality product targeted to true need and positioned by appeal to a higher discrimination in a certain group of consumers. She made the point that the current vacuum in this marketing approach actually suppressed "quality up-creep," acted as a lid, and that groups that risked exploring it would tap an upward spiral, an elevation.

A few in the audience expressed significant doubt. One repeated the mistaken impression that Lin was calling for the complete abandonment of stimulating sexual fear and arousal.

"No, I am not saying that," she countered. "But I do suggest that every time the urge to market to false machismo arises in your mind, you should hope a huge gong goes off in there and your mother's voice shouts in your ear, 'Detroit.' "

General laughs.

"How many people think my thesis is too soft, too naive? Honestly."

Seven of them raised their hands, one dramatically.

Lin confronted this with a sparkle in her eye.

"We must do better than that. How many think I am being too girlie?"

Laughter. All hands in the room shot up including five of the execs who were women. Henry Lane's hand was way up.

"Okay, okay. I can only assure you I am not coming primarily from goodness of feeling. I am coming from the most brutal regard for profit. Once again, a reminder, this morning Mr. Lane and I conducted a capital transaction in the amount of one point three billion dollars, and I am positive part of his trust in me and my bank in China is that we will deploy that money with the same brutal regard for profit."

"It's an understatement," threw in Lane.

Lin paused for emphasis. She took a step back. Her timing and delivery were perfect ...

"The sweet spot is above the waist."

There are several gasps and a drawn-in whistle of shock.

"It is a by-product that every individual of every persuasion will end up treated with more respect and that the culture will therefore benefit. That is a good thing. Personally, I am a proactive advocate for that. In fact, I have a side-bet with myself that tapping into this marketing niche can – well, not save the world – but can result in a better one. I don't care how girlie that sounds."

Laughs again.

"But my far over-arching focus is finding profit for this corporation. This approach is not a swap. It is an add-on.

"Let me say again, it is not necessary to leap over the chasm. Build a bridge. Gradually elevate. But the locus of persuasion has to become more and more the customer's rational, higher self, not the pit of the stomach or below the waist."

"Miss Lin, are you going to help us really clarify that? I can't speak for the others, but when you say the 'higher self' thing, I kind of feel it or see it, but not enough to nail it to the masthead for marketing and strategy. I need to be able to pin up a picture of this customer on the wall of our marketing and sales bullpen. Our guys there spit tobacco on the floor; this is not going to be easy."

"There is a technology. A social psychology technology. It can be used to find the customer, the niche and find the products that are amenable. I have less than an hour to go, but I have blocked out twenty minutes of that to explicate this technology. I will get to it in about fifteen minutes."

"Thank you."

"You used the word 'fake' in front of machismo. Is there 'un-fake?' "

" 'False.' Yes. Okay, I will use Detroit to illustrate. The love of machines, power, engineering. That heavy rumble that transmits through the transmission to the seat of the pants, right up the spine? Only genuine high quality product can do the trick. The true car lover knows the difference. The admiration comes from the higher self, the critical judgment that the rumble is real. That identification translates to an emotional, visceral, sexual feeling. Detroit used to have that at its foundation. The power of the World War II battleships and those huge guns got strapped to your muscle car's drive train. You won the war and saved the world with that rumble."

Lin paused to let that soak in.

"Who here owns a car like that?"

Two people raised their hands. She held eye contact with one of them.

"It's real."

"In the sixties, inflation, omissions controls, insurance penalties, these things made the real rumble too expensive or illegal. The true car lover bailed when things changed.

"But Detroit kept on selling the illusion of it, to men who could not detect the fakery that crept in, who wanted the jazz of the rumble without the reality of it, I call that false machismo. This is a limited, bankrupt policy, as we all observe, because fake rumble can't give you real sex."

"So Lin, you are not saying we should stop using sex to sell?"

"No, increase it tremendously. But the higher you aim above the waist, the better the orgasm."

"Can you give us an example?"

Lin picked up a small device. "Here is one. It is an Apple iPod. Brand new concept this year. I say 'concept' because it is both a piece of equipment and a system of management, customizing and delivery. I have all my music on mine. Now, there are other players, I believe they are called 'MP3 players,' but there is something about this iPod. It feels different. The experience of using it is different. You feel better about the world with this in your hand. I do not know where this is headed, but I wish Apple would do the same for these clunky mobile phones that they have done for this player."

Lin broke out into a demonstration of a certain little-known or favored consumer psychology study that was very different from the norm, was in fact the opposite: it searched for the niche repulsed by the emotional sale. She showed how this technology, combined with a smart philosophy of marketing, could open up her "add-on" profit center.

Lin continued her presentation.

"Well, I could talk about Detroit all day, it is such a perfect example. Now that I have shown you the technology of nailing up higher-self-man, I want to blow this up another ten thousand feet. What if I told you that this corporation could be at choice …" She stopped and looked over at Henry Lane.

"Miss Lin has my permission to pursue this topic. You should all have at it. Give it the A-class grilling."

"What if we could restructure some of the entities you

fund and run as follows: instead of being in bed with the government, sometimes warding off their agents, sometimes welcoming or encouraging regulation that we can survive, but our current competitors or future startups can not, to instead face the market naked, on direct appeal to quality and honest value only?"

"Jesus lady, I thought I was coming here to get a little training on the new company e-mail system."

Laughter. When it died out, Lin countered:

"I am extremely delighted to know I blew your girlie mind."

The best laughter yet.

"By the way, I Enjoy Being a Girl."

Whistles.

Then, with no preamble, Lin unleashed one of her stunners.

"When I return to the People's Republic of China next week, I will be getting on the plane with a billion of your money in my pocket. When I put that billion in play, it will be into a wide open, marginally-regulated, handshake and character-based free market cowboy banking system, and when we take our profits, we will pay not one cent in taxes."

Astounded silence greeted Lin's announcement. She held their stares proudly. For the remaining time afforded her, Lin explained the situation: this condition only existed because the Communists could not build the New China, so they engaged the entrepreneurs and agreed to stay at arm's length.

Her payoff: at the very end she painted a picture of the world where the United States would reverse its project against the free market and China would never go back to repressing it.

She rattled a few bones.

About the Author

Writer and composer John Caedan is passionate about portraying strivers in the throes of making visions come real. Inevitably this includes heat between men and women and the fascinating consequences when they turn their intensity on one another.

Mr. Caedan considers New York City and Southern California his neighborhood, yet his domicile is found at elevation 8140 in the Rocky Mountains, surrounded by special loved ones and a few pianos.

On the web: johncaedan.com
The music: thepreludes.com

www.ingramcontent.com/pod-product-compliance
Lightning Source LLC
Chambersburg PA
CBHW071302130626
46556CB00003B/1425